DEATH BY CARBS

PAIGE NICK

First published by N&B Books, 2015
Sales in Southern Africa by Bookstorm (www.bookstorm.co.za)
Distribution in the USA by Midpoint Trade

ISBN: 978-0-620-67435-5 (paperback)
ISBN: 978-0-620-67436-2 (e-book)

Editor: Helen Moffett
Proofreaders: Megan Clausen and Sophy Kohler
Cover design: Karin Barry-McCormack
Typesetting: Reneé Naudé

This book is dedicated to anyone who has ever struggled
to lose weight, and knows how murderous it can be.

THE COP

A cop who liked donuts: he was the world's biggest cliché. Bennie September turned on the interior light in the car and angled the rear-view mirror so he could catch a glimpse of his face. Then he swept back and forth at his top lip with his fingertips. It wasn't easy getting powdered sugar out of a moustache.

He dropped the now-empty cardboard Pick 'n Pay box on the floor of the passenger seat of his old Opel, then strained against the seatbelt to shove the box as far back under the seat as possible. That was the first rule for anyone committing a crime, wasn't it? Get rid of the evidence. He could hear the box knocking against the empty Coke and Fanta Orange cans, which he'd hidden under the seat earlier. Exhibits B, C, D and E.

Bennie wiped his hands down the front of his jacket and swore as he transplanted white streaks of powdered sugar from his fingertips onto his lapels. He swore again, unclipped his seat belt, pulled off his jacket, balled it up and tossed it onto the back seat, which was littered with newspapers. If Felicia found that donut box and those cans, he'd be sleeping on the couch for weeks. But at least the mystery of why his wife was losing weight at a rate of knots, and he wasn't, would be solved. Shame, he felt quite bad about it, she was genuinely baffled. She swore by this new Banting diet, and had banished all carbs and sugar from their home. Puzzled when this didn't work for him, she'd cut down his dairy intake and increased his fats even further, but with no joy, and she couldn't figure out why. The answer was simple, really: gatsbys.

He checked his moustache in the rear-view mirror again before getting out the car. He used to keep count of the crime scenes, but he gave that up when he hit triple digits. These days, there were more crime scenes in South Africa than non-crime scenes.

But this one was different. A celebrity had been assaulted. Professor Tim Noakes, the diet guru. Bennie nodded at the team of cops lurking outside the front of Noakes's large, leafy property in Constantia, cordoning off the area.

'Evening,' Bennie greeted two of the policemen standing closest to the front gate.

'Morning,' one of the cops responded.

Bennie looked at his watch; the cop was right, the little hand was on three and the big hand was on half-past exhaustion and overtime. 'Okay, gents, let's do what we can to keep the media's noses out of this one for as long as possible. This case is going to be hot.'

'We got it covered, Detective,' the other policeman said.

If only, Bennie thought. Police communications weren't safe anymore; there was always someone listening in, or filming stuff on their cell phone and leaking it online, even selling it to a magazine or newspaper for a pile of cash. He'd bet money that a squeeze or cousin of the dispatch agent who'd taken the emergency call when the attack had first been reported had already updated their Facebook status with the news.

Hard to believe a dieting guru could be such a huge deal. But celebrity didn't mean so much here. In South Africa, a celebrity could be someone with more than five thousand followers on Twitter, or a beat-boxer who got kicked out of *Idols* in round two, or even a blogger who ranted about mommy issues. When you don't have a lot to look up to, you don't end up looking very high.

As Bennie entered the property, he spotted the EMS team hurrying out of the house towards him with a body on a gurney.

'That him?' he asked as they walk-ran the gurney towards the ambulance. He squinted at the body through the gloom. The victim appeared to be in his sixties. He had a slim build and even prone, Bennie could tell he was tall, definitely over six feet. He was wearing a black knitted beanie, a long-sleeved, dark-blue sweatshirt, black jeans and a pair of takkies. His lined face was a mask of blood.

The EMTs nodded.

'And?' Bennie asked the one closest to him. He didn't recognise either of them – they looked barely out of their teens. He knew most of the Metro Ambulance guys – they were all in it together, this shitty daily grind of blood and guts – but these two must be new.

The younger of the two glanced nervously at his companion, then blurted: 'He's um … bleeding from the nose and…'

The other one, looking exhausted, filled in, his words racing. 'White male, head injuries, potential head trauma. He has a faint pulse, but he's in critical condition. Sir, problem is…'

'Detective,' Bennie corrected him.

'Detective, problem is,' the EMT said as he pulled open the back of the ambulance, 'a bus collided with a truck on the N1 about an hour ago. It's a real mess, so we're on skeleton crew and vehicles here. Which means we don't have the equipment or, to be honest, the expertise to deal with him.'

'We need to get him to the hospital stat,' said the other kid as they fed the gurney into the ambulance.

Bennie rolled his eyes. These kids watched too much *Grey's Anatomy* – no doctor in South Africa ever actually said 'stat'. He watched the ambulance – which had seen better days – tear down the street, cornering practically on two wheels, siren blaring, red lights flashing. Between budget cuts, uncontrolled short-staffing and corruption, it was a miracle anyone made it out alive these days.

THE PARAMEDICS

S'bu's roar from the back of the ambulance could only mean one thing, and it wasn't good. Zayne risked a glance back over his shoulder and saw S'bu, slumped, shaking his head. Zayne turned back to keep his eye on the road – the ambulance handled like a tank, and he needed to concentrate.

'Everything okay back there, bru?' he called.

'I did everything I could,' S'bu yelled back.

'I know you did,' Zayne said.

'You should probably turn off the siren.'

'Howcome?'

'Well, we're not in a hurry anymore. He's already late.'

Zayne turned off the siren and drove in silence for a minute. He didn't know what to say.

'Pull over,' S'bu instructed, 'and I'll come join you up front. Then we should probably do a U-ey.'

'Howcome?' Zayne said.

'The morgue's in the other direction.'

THE COP

Once he'd seen the ambulance off, Bennie chatted to the cops outside Noakes's house and made a few notes in the pocket-sized notebook he always kept with him. Then he stepped through the front door and followed the sound of a camera lens clicking towards the kitchen, where a crime scene photographer was recording the room at every angle, his shoes shod in standard-issue crime-scene booties.

'Slim,' Bennie greeted him. The photographer's shift must have finished an hour ago, and it was unlikely in current circumstances that the man would be paid overtime. Bennie didn't know how or why these guys put up with it.

'Howzit, Bennie,' Slim said, nodding soberly, then returning to his viewfinder. They'd seen each other three hours earlier: similar scene, different location.

The chairs around the kitchen table had been knocked over, and the glass door leading from outside into the kitchen was wide open. The handle had been neatly removed, clearly so that someone could gain entry. There were splinters of a shattered UCT-branded mug on the floor, and something spilled and pooled around it – tea, perhaps. Bennie also took note of the blood spatters across the kitchen counter, some on the floor and on the back of a chair, as well as bloodied handprints against the wall.

A man in a bulletproof vest, a large crested logo and the words Jabulani Security printed on it, appeared through a second door that connected the kitchen to a formal lounge.

'Hey,' Bennie said, nodding at the Jabulani guard.

'Hey, Detective,' the guard said back.

Private security companies were big business in South Africa. Just about every middle-class home and most businesses were linked to an alarm or carefully placed emergency buttons, which were in turn linked to a security company call centre. Bennie had done the maths and often wondered if he was in the wrong business. Maybe it's what he would do one day when he was ready to retire – if he made it that far without a triple bypass or a fatal stab wound.

'Who called it in?' Bennie asked.

'The domestic worker, her name is Gloria Ngeju. She pressed the panic button at 2:50am. She had just come back from a three-week trip to the Eastern Cape for a funeral. The bus had broken down for several hours en route, so she was very late getting home. When she arrived, she noticed the back door was open, and looked in. She saw her boss lying over there, face down on the floor. And then she saw the blood. She screamed, ran to her flat at the back of the property and locked herself in, scared the attacker was still in the house. Then she pressed the alarm button. I was first on the scene and I called it in to our dispatch, who called the police and the ambulance.'

'Where's the rest of the family?' Bennie asked.

'There was nobody else here. There's a wife; neighbours say they're always together. She's not here, and nobody has been able to get hold of her,' the security guard said. 'But it is the middle of the night, so maybe she has her phone off wherever she is, or something? Or maybe they kidnapped her? Burglary gone wrong?'

'Maybe,' Bennie said, and made a few more notes. Everyone thought they were a detective these days. He blamed it on all the cop shows on TV. 'Did … er … Mrs Ngeju say if anything's been stolen from the house, if anything important has been moved, perhaps, or broken?' he asked.

'She's not sure, but she's very shaken and quite hysterical. She's been working for the family for twelve years. The EMS guys gave her something to calm her down. There were also a lot of neighbours here.

They must have come when they heard her screaming. So I sent them home, to try keep the crime scene as clean as possible.'

'Great, thanks, good job,' Bennie said. Christ, nosy neighbours, that's just what he needed. 'You know what the press is like with celebrities. We're going to have them and a bunch of lawyers crawling up our arses in about a minute.'

'Who is he?' the security guard asked.

Bennie stepped carefully around the broken mug and crouched down so he could examine the markings indicating where the body had been found. He felt his belt stretch and divide his boep as he bent.

'Professor Tim Noakes,' Bennie said.

'That diet guy?'

'That's the one.'

The security guard whistled. 'Who would want to hurt that oke?'

'I reckon there's probably a queue. Hell, I've been wanting to kill him myself for months,' Bennie said, rising back up to his full height and adjusting his waistband. Bending down like that was too uncomfortable.

'Hey, has anyone seen the fingerprinting guy yet?' Bennie called out.

'He just called,' the photographer said. 'He said he's having a problem, but he's coming as fast as he can.'

'What kind of problem?'

'Something to do with load-shedding.'

THE PARAMEDICS

Zayne felt like he was going to be sick. Bile rose in his throat, and saliva pooled in his mouth. He buzzed opened his window and breathed in big gulps of air as he drove along the highway towards town.

'You okay, bru?' S'bu asked from the passenger seat.

Zayne nodded.

'Your first dead body?'

He nodded again, worried that if he opened his mouth to speak, he wouldn't be able to stop the bile from coming up.

'You'll get used to it,' S'bu said. 'Just take deep breaths. Do you want me to drive?'

'Nah, I'll be fine,' Zayne managed to get out.

'It gets easier. Well, it doesn't, but you'll get better at dealing with it.'

'How long have you been doing this?' Zayne asked.

'Five nights.'

They drove along in silence for a few moments.

'If you don't mind me asking, what made you decide to become a paramedic?' S'bu asked, breaking the silence. 'No offence, it's just you seem a bit squeamish, and you know in this job...' he trailed off.

'My mom really wanted me to be a doctor. But I wasn't so great at school, so this was kind of the next best thing,' Zayne said.

There was no moon, so they drove along the highway in silence through dark pockets of night, both lost in their thoughts. Zayne thought about the once-living, now-dead man in the back of the ambulance, and the choices that had brought him to the front seat of an ambulance in the early hours of the morning. He was young and bright;

he could have gone into PR, or been a teacher, or anything. Maybe even a model: his mom and aunts were constantly telling him how handsome he was. To say he was having major regrets would be an understatement, and this was only his first night on the job.

'S'bu, do you think if we had better equipment, or someone more experienced riding along with us, we could have saved him?'

S'bu looked out the window and took a minute before he answered.

'Maybe,' he said quietly. 'I did absolutely everything I knew how to do.'

'I know you did, bru,' Zayne said as he came to a stop at a dead traffic light on Main Road, Salt River, checking carefully for cross-traffic.

'Out, out, out! Don't make me hurt you! Turn off the engine and get out, and no funny business or I'll shoot you!' A voice shouted through the open window, deafening Zayne, flying spit flecking his cheek. He lifted his foot off the brake in shock and the ambulance shuddered and stalled. Before he could think or move, Zayne felt the ambulance door give beside him, cold air rushing in, and he froze as the man climbed up next to him, the smell of his sweat overwhelming. Cold metal pressed against his forehead. He closed his eyes and swallowed hard. You never knew how you would react in a situation like this until it happened, and clearly his default reaction was paralysis.

In what felt like slow motion, Zayne was yanked from the driver's seat by his sleeve and thrown to the pavement. He heard S'bu shout out, and in his peripheral vision he caught sight of his partner crumpling in the passenger seat, hit or shot, Zayne couldn't tell. As he pulled himself into a sitting position on the street, the thought crossed his mind that once all this was over, if he was still alive and S'bu was hurt, and he called for an ambulance, they probably wouldn't have one to send. These cutbacks were going to kill them all.

Zayne watched, his vision blurred by panic, as the man in the driver's seat turned on the ignition. S'bu must have also been hauled out the ambulance, because there was now another man in a leatherette jacket climbing up into the passenger seat.

'Thanks,' the driver said to Zayne, a casual smile on his face. Then before the other guy had even closed the passenger door, the ambulance was skidding off down the road, the rear end fishtailing for a moment, then righting itself as it disappeared out of sight.

'Zayne, are you okay?' S'bu shouted across the road.

Zayne staggered to his feet, bent over and vomited his guts up in the middle of the road. This was not how he'd pictured his first night in his new job.

THE HIJACKERS

Papsak rifled through the cubbyhole in the ambulance as Thabo hurtled down the highway towards Epping Industria.

'Anything in there?' Thabo asked.

Papsak pulled out a wad of papers and paged through them, tossing the ones that didn't interest him out the window, along with a few empty chip packets. He kept the manual and the ambulance's papers to one side, then went back to fishing in the cubbyhole. He brought out a black peak cap embroidered with the SuperSport logo, dusted it off, turned it around, and put it on.

'Nuh-uh, Thabs,' he said, as he fished around in the other pockets in the ambulance door, then felt under the seat. Finally he reached round into the spaces behind both their seats.

'Look properly, don't miss anything … no gun, no knife? You sure?' the driver asked.

Papsak shook his head.

'Not bad, hey?' said Thabo, patting the steering wheel. 'Only ninety-seven thousand on the clock. Moe should give us more than five grand for this; it's a major find. Five grand's a rip-off.'

Papsak paged through the vehicle's manual. 'Nxaa, slow down,' he snapped. 'If we get pulled over, Moe will kill us slowly.'

Thabo pulled the ambulance into the back of the workshop and waited for the garage door to close all the way before he turned off the engine, and they both climbed out.

'Check out the back,' Thabo said.

'Why don't you check out the back?' Papsak spat.

Thabo rolled his eyes at his friend, then went round to the back of the ambulance, Papsak close behind him. They hauled open the doors and both scrambled in.

'Fok!' Thabo shouted.

'But … but … they weren't driving with any sirens or lights on. How were we supposed to know there was anyone in here?' Papsak asked.

Thabo leaned over to get a closer look at the body. 'Shit!' he said. 'You'd better go get Moe.'

THE CO-AUTHORS

Marco's tummy had been gurgling and churning ever since he'd snuck in just after three that morning. He'd had a stingingly hot shower and crawled into bed as quietly as possible so as to not wake Chris. His nonna used to call those sounds tummy goblins.

He lay watching his beautiful husband breathing evenly in the bed beside him. He was so lucky: he was with this phenomenal man, he was the co-author of a successful book, with another one on the way, he had his own restaurant, and now the man standing between him and household-name fame was dead. The body had only just been found and the internet was already exploding with news and rumours. He should be happy. So then why couldn't he sleep? Was it guilt? He owed so much to the dead man.

The restaurant was half the problem. When he'd first opened the Banting Bistro, he thought it would be packed from morning till midnight. Hundreds of thousands of South Africans had embraced the Banting lifestyle, after all. But he'd learnt the hard way that it wasn't always that simple, and running a niche restaurant was a fool's errand. The way things were going, he had barely enough to keep the restaurant afloat for another couple of months – and only thanks to his share of the royalties from the Real Meal Revolution book – and then he was going to have to consider closing down. Unless of course, this new book of Mediterranean Banting recipes shot to the top of the bestseller lists, and him being the face of it helped turn the restaurant around. It was his only hope.

His stomach gurgled again. He gave up on sleep, snuck out of bed and tiptoed down to the kitchen.

Marco kneaded the dough by hand, the way his nonna and her nonna before her, and *her* nonna before her, used to back in Italy. The methods were identical; only the ingredients were different. Not eggs from the back garden, or home-milled flour, or butter from freshly milked, grass-fed, free-to-roam cows, but the local equivalents from Oranjezicht City Farm instead.

He wiped his forehead with floury fingers, getting clods of dough stuck in his thick black hair. He ignored them and went back to kneading. He didn't know of a more contemplative or therapeutic pastime. Once the dough was in the fridge, he heaved his nonna's ancient stainless-steel pasta machine out of the cupboard and set it up on the counter, before turning on the stove to bring a pot of lightly salted water with a splash of extra-virgin olive oil to the boil. He ran his hand over the cool steel of the pasta maker. It weighed a ton, and was as solid as a battleship. They didn't make things like this anymore.

While Marco's homemade pasta came to the boil, he whipped up a basil pesto, using fresh pine kernels and leaves he had picked from the potted basil on the windowsill, one by one.

He drained his al dente pasta into the sink, then dished up a large bowl of it, spooned in the pesto, grated in shavings off a large wedge of Parmesan, and finished it with pinches of Maldon salt, fresh parsley from another pot on the windowsill, and a couple of turns of pepper from a large wooden grinder he and Chris had received as a wedding present.

Marco settled at the kitchen counter, dug his fork into the bowl and gave the pasta a twirl, wrapping it around his fork, and scooping it into his mouth with the aid of a spoon, Italian-style. Once he'd finished the first bowl, he dished up a second, and then a third, and finally a fourth bowl. This time he didn't bother sitting down; he stood beside the Smeg, dug his fork in, twirled the pasta around it and leaned against the cool brushed-steel refrigerator, shovelling the pasta into his mouth as tears poured down his cheeks, marking trails through the flour that dusted his face. He slid down the fridge and landed on the black-and-white chequered kitchen floor, sobbing, the half-empty bowl lying in his lap, the fresh pasta turning flabby.

Marco was crying so loudly, he didn't hear the footsteps until Chris was bending down beside him.

'Oh honey,' Chris said gently, taking the bowl from him, 'not again.'

THE FANS

THE BANTING FOR LIFE FACEBOOK PAGE

Deborah Gogh
I have terrible news for all my Banting friends and fans on this page. I just read on Twitter that Professor Tim Noakes died after an attack in his home in the early hours of this morning.

Phillip Stewart Is this somce kind of joke? Because if it is its not funny.
Like 46

Melissa Giles It's true. I went to go look on Twitter. How did he die? Does anyone know any other information or circumstances? My condolences go out to us and his family.
Like 12

Borrie Human HOW? WHAT! THIS CANT' BE! I DONT'UNDERSTAND
Like 19

Deborah Gogh From what I can see on Twitter, the police haven't yet released a statement. It's such sad news. I just can't believe it. I was reading his book only this morning, it's become my bible.
Like 42

Margie Oosthuizen Do they know how he died?
Like 2

Murray Bruvick I hope he didn't have a heart attack!!
Like 31

Charte Tonder That would be really bad!
Like 19

Kwela McKaiser They're saying he was murdered and there's some pictures of face full of blood from someone's cell phone on the scene which is very blurry. But it hasn't been confirmed by the authorities yet.
Like 21

Murray Bruvick Phew, as long as he didn't have a heart attack!!
Like 19

Joanne Sloanne My condonlenses go out to his whole family. This is tragic. I feel like I've lost a close friend. We are praying for you all.
Like 12

Maureen Ewehout I can't believe what I'm reading. Ever since my husband died, this group and Banting have saved me. I've lost more than 27 kilograms, and I feel like at the age of 60 I've finally found my calling and my purpose in life, thanks to The Real Meal Revolution. I've made so many new friends. This is the worst news I've heard since my husband's passing. Tim Noakes was my very good friend. Just before he died, we worked together on some Marvellous Tim Noakes ENDORSED Real Meal Revolution Meal Plans. Get yours for just R150 each. Direct message me to find out more. It's terrible news, but in his honour we should all dedicate ourselves to his incredible, life-changing, world-beating diet plan, with the help of my Marvellous Tim Noakes ENDORSED meal plans.
Like 8

Bernard Lewis I know me too. He's done so much for me. Banting has changed my life. Ive also lost a whopping 24 kilograms since January and Im speeding towards my goal wait. I've tried every diet known to mankind my whole life, and nothing has ever worked for me before. Without the Prof, I'd probably still literly be eating myself to death.
Like 35

Sheena Easting Hi **Maureen Ewehout** your diet plans does sound interesting. Are they really endorsed by the Prof himself?
Like 3

Maureen Ewehout Hello **Sheena Easting** yes, I met the good Professor at a Banting conference in Balito 18 months ago, and we've been working intensely on these meal plans together for the last four to five months. We were going to launch them soon. But with this tragic news of his death, I know he would have wanted me to launch them now, to keep his work alive. Message me if you'd like your very own Marvellous Tim Noakes ENDORSED meal plans, for just R150 each.
Like 4

Deedee Wolhutter Hey everyone, join me in a celebration of a great man's life. Let's each one of us light a candle tonight and put it in our windows in honour of the great professor, who has touched so many lives, and changed the way we think about food and about bacon.
Like 28

Dot Swart Hello, are candles on the green list?
Like 2

Doug Larter That has to be the most ignorant comment of the day, Dot Swart
Like 11

Dot Swart No Doug Larter, I mean that candles are made of wax, and isnt that made from bees and honey? And all Im saying is that if honey is on the Red or Orange list, then I just think that to honor the professor and all his work, and how hes changed our lives forever, then we shuddnt use them.
Like 15

Pauline Oppelt Honey is on the Orange List. You're allowed one spoon of it a day, so I don't know if we should do the whole candle thing or not.
Like 22

Donna Kirsch Maybe just half a candle?
Like 22

Shana Kurz Hello clever banting people ... a question about psyllium husk – do you know, can you tell me is there a difference between all the products, are some better than others ... or are all psyllium husk brands pretty much the same?
Like 0
View 1267 more comments

The Professor's death had been an unfortunate necessity, Maureen Ewehout thought, as she typed her sales pitch into the Banting for Life Facebook Page and then pressed 'post'.

Her idea was pure genius: Tim Noakes ENDORSED meal plans. Surely there would be a huge demand for them now, and of course, with him having died so unexpectedly, nobody could really question their validity, could they? It would be a 'he said, she said' thing, and she could easily manufacture proof of correspondence between them if she absolutely had to, you could do anything on the internet these days. Nobody had a signature or handwriting sample online, everybody's voice was a standard Helvetica nine points, and it was as easy as Banting-friendly pie to recreate that.

Maureen was totally safe. Nobody would ever know that the Prof had never even heard of her. It was inspired. Her inbox was already pinging with messages from interested Banters.

She took out her laptop cleaning spray and wiped her screen and keyboard with the blue purpose-made cloth. To think that two years ago she didn't even own a laptop, and now it was the last thing she looked at before she closed her eyes at night, and the first thing she touched when she opened them the next morning. What did the kids call it these days? FOMO, fear of missing out. She'd learnt what that was on Urban Dictionary – online of course. Maureen had FOMO: she didn't want to miss a thing online.

But then there was a lot about her that had changed over the last couple of years. The most visible being her weight. Seventeen kilograms off in her first year of Banting, another ten in her second, and she'd plateaued at around the weight she was when she'd married Gus, thirty-eight years ago. Pity he didn't live long enough to see the day when at sixty, she could fit into the wedding dress she'd worn at twenty-two. She'd pulled it out of the attic when she reached her goal weight, and it had fitted like a (slightly old-fashioned) glove.

The sad part was that if Gus were still alive today, she probably wouldn't have ever embarked on this journey in the first place. It was the loneliness that had set the whole thing in motion, along with her only son, who'd bought her the laptop before he and his wife emigrated to New Zealand, so they could 'stay in touch'.

First Maureen had found a couple of old friends on Facebook, and then she'd stumbled across the Banting for Life Facebook group. She'd never even heard of the lifestyle before, and at that time the group had twelve thousand members. In the time she'd been following it, membership had grown to a hundred thousand people. It felt as if almost everyone in South Africa was getting in on the action in some way or other. They were talking about Banting in the queue at the pharmacy, and even at the weekly aqua aerobics class she'd started going to down at the gym once she'd lost enough weight to be able to get into a swimming costume.

Everyone on the Banting for Life Facebook group was so friendly and encouraging. After her first few weeks of silently following the activity on the page, she'd finally built up enough courage to 'like' the occasional post. Eventually she had started commenting herself, and now her timeline was full of Banting chat.

At first, it was all the cheery success stories that had helped her overcome her shyness. So many people losing twenty, thirty, even forty kilograms in only a matter of months, and they all seemed to enjoy it so much, enthusiastically sharing their recipes and ideas. She could still remember her first post on the page, verbatim:

That was nearly two years earlier, and the support had been overwhelmingly positive and inspirational. And what a revelation the Real Meal Revolution was – it went against everything Maureen had ever believed about nutrition. In this new world, up was down and down was up. Fat was good – whatever next?

The Professor had been a genius, and she would definitely light a candle in his honour tonight, regardless of whether honey was on the orange list or not. It was an awful shame he had to die, she thought as she hefted the knobkierie off the kitchen counter, washed it carefully under the hot tap, dried it and put it back behind the kitchen door where it belonged. The Banting community would miss him terribly. But sadly, his death was the only way her little business would ever thrive. That's life for you: full of sacrifices and quite bittersweet – even without any sugar in it.

THE HIJACKERS

'I didn't ask for a body,' Moe said. He was taller and fatter than both Thabo and Papsak. He stood behind the ambulance with his hands on his hips. His massive head was closely shaven and he had a curved pillow of fat, almost a second head, which rolled along the nape of his neck, giving his oversized bald kop something to lean on. He was not someone you wanted to mess with when he was in a good mood, and right now, having been woken and dragged from his bed far too early, he was not in a good mood.

'I said bring me an ambulance, not bring me an ambulance and a dead body. You two skelms couldn't organise tik in Lavender Hill.' He sucked on his teeth and scratched his protruding belly with one finger, giving them a narrow-eyed look before reaching into his back pocket and pulling out two wads of cash. He handed one to Papsak, and gave the other to Thabo.

Thabo flipped slowly through his wad. 'I thought you said five large, Moe?'

'I did,' Moe said.

'There's nowhere near that much here.'

'Two and a half for you, and two and a half for umhlobo wakho,' Moe said, pointing at each of them and speaking slowly as if they were both dimwits. 'That equals five. And you should consider yourselves lucky that you're getting any of it. Look at this old skadonk and the mess you've made of this job. That body is going to make this ambulance hotter than Bonang. They'll have to make an investigation, and this body's family is going to be looking for him. So unless you want me to get another ambulance to take you two fuck-ups away in, you'd better take your body and your money and voetsek!'

'But what are we supposed to do with the body?' Papsak asked.

'Not my body, not my problem,' shrugged Moe as he turned and waddled to his office at the back of the warehouse. 'But you've got twenty minutes to get yourselves and him out of here.'

THE CEO

Not a day went by that Trevor didn't wish he'd gone into bacon. People would always like bacon, wouldn't they? Most of them, anyway. Not the Jews and Muslims of course, although some of them seemed to be coming around to it.

Earlier that morning, Trevor had considered the road paint business; people would always need road paint. Well, as long as there were roads. And before that, in the changing room at the gym, he'd eagerly considered the towel business (although he would definitely make them bigger, he thought – everybody made towels too small these days). There was also the running shoe business, and at this point, even the showerhead business seemed attractive. Surely those industries would be less stressful than the one he was in right now? Hell, working as head of public relations at Eskom would be less stressful.

It wasn't even eight am yet, and Trevor had already weighed up at least ten different career alternatives to being the Managing Director of a company that manufactured bread, baked goods and snacks.

It was sheer dumb luck that he'd managed to find his way into a dying industry. What an idiot. These days, carbs were the enemy. Bread sales had taken a serious beating as a result, and were at an all-time low. When Trevor had first started out as VP of sales at SnackCorp, seven years earlier, it had been the heyday of bread. Carbs were king. They'd all cruised to some exotic destination for their annual corporate bosberaad to play golf and pat each other on the back. Company life was a year-round, all-you-could-eat buffet of prawns, strippers, congratulations, narcissism and booze. And carbs. Truckloads of carbs.

But not anymore. Sales figures had plummeted, stocks had hit rock bottom, and the board was tightening belts left, right and centre. And now, three mass retrenchments later, they were still running scared and pointing fingers. Unless Trevor came up with something fast, it looked like they were going to use him as the next scapegoat. Trim the fat (ironically), lose the dead weight. And then what? Who in South Africa was going to hire a short, short-sighted, slightly overweight, fifty-six-year-old white man?

Trevor needed this job; he had his ex-wife's maintenance to cover. And what about his Merc, and the penthouse? Trevor scratched at his balding scalp, then self-consciously tried to rearrange the wisps of hair that remained. It didn't help that SnackCorp had a forty-nine per cent shareholding in the Central Soda Company. Sugar *and* carbs: just great. He'd backed the only two lame donkeys in a horse race. Why hadn't he gone into the xylitol business instead? Then life would be sweet. But he had a plan, and he felt a warm surge of hope as he considered it. If all went well, an upturn was imminent.

Trevor picked up a piece of toast off his plate and examined both sides of it. It was a slice of SnackCorp's low-GI wholewheat, and it was perfectly toasted on one side, but slightly overdone (read: burnt) on the other. He checked that his office door was closed, then pulled a brown paper bag out from the bottom drawer of his desk, and slipped the piece of toast into it. He put the second piece in after it, folded the lip of the bag and placed the sack on the edge of his desk to deal with later. Then he tucked into the rest of his breakfast from the office canteen: eggs, bacon, tomato, mushrooms and avocado.

That fucking Real Meal Revolution or Banting, as people had taken to calling it, was killing him slowly and saving his life quickly – at the same time.

Here he was, on the verge of a ruined career, potential homeless-ness and Mercedes-lessness on the one hand; but on the other, he'd lost twenty-five kilos in under a year – thanks to Banting. He still had another fifteen kilos to go before he reached his goal weight, but he had to admit it was working for him. He felt lighter, healthier and more energetic than he had in years, plus his eczema had magically cleared up. Whenever anyone asked what his weight-loss secret was, he attributed it to the running and swimming he now had to do every day at the gym as part of his carefully constructed cover-up. But in truth, he knew it was that fucking diet; the very thing that was slowly strangling his company and hanging him out to dry.

He'd started the whole thing out of curiosity more than anything else. He'd created a fake profile on Facebook with the intention of following a few of the Banting groups that were becoming more and more popular. He considered it research. Classic Sun Tzu strategy from that famous book, *The Art of War*. Know your enemy and your customer and your rivals, and all that nonsense. He needed to know what people were saying about his products. He'd also wanted to prove to the nervous nagging voice in his head that Banting was just another fad that would soon pass. But that had been well over a year ago. And he'd slowly been sucked into all these people's posts. Their highs and lows and triumphs and failures – and the spats too, of course. People seemed to lose all manners and judgement once they had a monitor as a barrier between themselves and real life. But the overwhelming truth he'd discovered was that there seemed to be so much weight being lost by so many people. Thousands of fans who were evangelical in their belief in this lifestyle, with the before-and-after selfies by the bucket-load to prove their success. These posts had become irresistible to Trevor, whose belt had been stretched out beyond recognition by all those good bread years at SnackCorp.

And so shortly after he joined the Banting for Life group, he'd decided to try Banting for himself, in secret of course (the b-word was strictly banned at SnackCorp). Motivated partly by research, partly fear, and partly simply the size of his gut.

Trevor sifted through the morning papers as he ate his breakfast, mopping up the last of the yolk with a piece of bacon as he worked his way through *Business Day* and every column inch of depression it brought with it. His spirits sagged as he scanned SnackCorp's plummeting shares. He hadn't thought they could get much lower than the previous week's dismal showing, but this morning they had exceeded all his worst fears.

Of course there were other factors involved, one being the one-million ton drop in maize supplies in the last year. The drought in the Free State and North West had caused irreparable damage to maize prices and consumption in South Africa. But one of the biggest factors impacting on sales of bread, rice and similar products was, without a doubt, coming directly from the top end of the market. A drought would eventually end, rain would come as it always did, and maize would grow, but the more serious issue was these Banting converts. They were growing in size and power daily, and once they stopped buying ninety-eight per cent of SnackCorp's products, and began seeing the positive results, they were unlikely ever to return to their former purchasing habits – and when these people went, they were taking their families with them. His target market was literally shrinking. He'd had to man up and do something about it. He'd had no choice.

When Trevor was done with the papers, he turned to his laptop and logged on to Facebook. It was his morning ritual: the bad news first, scouring the papers and the stock prices, and when that was finished, over to Facebook, which always cheered him up. The irony of how much he enjoyed the Banting groups that were doing his business in wasn't lost on him. He navigated straight to the Banting for Life page, and scrolled through the posts and comments that had been added since he'd been online the night before.

He yelped, then covered his mouth with his hand. He shot to his feet, his chair rolling back along the floor. Still standing, now leaning over his computer, Trevor went to Google and typed in Noakes's name. He scrolled carefully through every relevant piece of news he could find, his mouth dry.

The phone on his desk rang, but he ignored it. Then his cell phone rang. He ignored that, too. When it finally cut off, the phone on his desk started ringing again. He reached into his pocket and pulled out the pager he'd bought last month. Ancient technology, but perfect for his purposes. There were no new messages. Still ignoring the bleating phone on his desk, Trevor snatched up the brown paper bag and hurried out his office and down the green-carpeted passageway. The feng shui office design consultants, who'd cost him a hundred k just two years ago, said that green would have a 'calming effect' on his employees and 'would boost productivity.' Well, he wasn't bloody well feeling very calm right now. He pressed the lift button and shifted from foot to foot as he jingled the change in his pocket. Someone from sales greeted him, but he didn't reply. He rose on his tiptoes, and then dropped back down again while he waited for the lift. He pressed the button four or five more times, knowing that it wouldn't bring the lift any faster, but needing to give his trembling fingers something to do.

THE HIJACKERS

'You take his head and I'll take his feet,' Thabo said.

'Why do I have to take his head? You take his head, I'll take his feet,' Papsak whined.

'Fine,' Thabo sighed, 'you take his fucking feet then.'

'Fok, why's he so bliksem heavy?' Papsak swore.

'He's dead, not empty,' Thabo said through gritted teeth as they heaved the body out the ambulance and laid him on the floor of the workshop.

'He's just some old mlungu,' Thabo said, pulling the beanie off the dead man's head. 'Check his pockets.'

'Why do I always have to do everything, why don't *you* check his pockets? I'm smoking,' grumbled Papsak, stepping back and lighting a roll-up.

Thabo clicked his tongue, then knelt next to the body and rifled through the dead man's front pockets, pulling a face when all he came up with was a small blue sweet in clear wrapping with the Spur logo on it, and a toothpick in the right pocket. He got luckier with the left front pocket, where he found a cell phone. He examined the Samsung, which had a fully charged battery and no missed calls, then slipped it into the inside pocket of his jacket before calling Papsak back over.

'Help me turn him over,' he shouted.

The two men turned the mlungu over and Thabo felt in his back pockets, pulling a wad of cash out of the left-hand one. He whistled slowly, and then sat back on his heels to count the money.

'How much is it?' Papsak asked, moving in closer.

'Oh, now you're interested, tyhini!' Thabo said.

'How much? It looks like a lot.'

'Give me a second.' Thabo counted furiously. 'It is a lot. It's like, like, like...'

'Yes?' said Papsak, breathing down Thabo's neck.

'It's ten grand,' Thabo said after he'd taken his time and counted it twice.

'Yohhhhhh!' Papsak said, doing pantsula on the spot. 'With the five grand we got from Moe, we'll definitely be able to buy the gusheshe from Lefty now.'

'At last, my friend. Tonight we drive!' Thabo grinned.

'Hamba, we'd better go get the gusheshe before Lefty sells it to someone else,' Papsak said.

Thabo folded the wad and stowed it in his inside pocket next to his new cell phone. Then the two men fist-bumped.

'Wait, what are we going to do with him?' Papsak asked, nudging the body with his toe.

They stood peering at it, the mood suddenly serious.

'I don't know. I've never had to get rid of a dead mlungu before,' Thabo said.

'Dump him, maybe?' Papsak asked.

'Where?'

'I don't know. On the street out there?'

'In Epping industria? No way! What if someone sees us?' Thabo said. 'There are cameras everywhere now. Haven't you seen Big Brother?'

'No, bhuti, you know I haven't got a dish at home. Have you got any better ideas?'

'Why don't we take him with us to Lefty's? We can buy the gusheshe and ask Lefty what to do. He's a man who knows how to get things done.'

'Maybe he'll even buy the mlungu from us to sell for muti or something. Then we'll have even more clips.'

Thabo nodded slowly. 'But how will we get him to Lefty's shebeen?

He weighs like an elephant. Do you know anyone with a car?'

Papsak shook his head.

'What about your Uncle Sifiso?'

'No way!' Papsak shouted. 'He'll tell Mama, and she'll turn me inside out. Then you'll have two bodies to deal with.'

'Well then, how are we supposed to get him to Lefty's?' Thabo asked.

'Taxi?'

THE CEO

Trevor walked a few blocks from the SnackCorp headquarters, then ducked into an alleyway. He checked over both shoulders to make sure nobody was following him, then dropped the brown paper bag with the two slices of toast into the stinking bins at the back of a Chinese restaurant. If anyone discovered him turfing their flagship product back at the office, he'd be in big trouble. Looking to make sure nobody had seen him, he returned to the street.

Instead of going back towards his office, he walked in the opposite direction, casting constant anxious backward glances.

He finally reached the public telephone booth he'd scouted out a month ago, when he'd first started planning this thing. It had been harder to find a public payphone than he had thought. Very few remained in any big city these days, and the few that could be found were broken or had been vandalised. Nowadays everyone had cell phones. Public phones represented old, unloved technology – only useful for someone who needed to make an illicit call, and didn't want to leave a paper trail by RICA-ing a cheap cell phone. Someone like Trevor.

He picked up the receiver, slipped a coin into the slot, checked over his shoulder once more, then dialed the number he'd taken care to memorise. His adrenalin surged, and for a moment he thought he might lose his barely digested LCHF breakfast.

The number rang and rang and rang, until finally a robotic voice message kicked in: 'The person you have dialled is not available at present; please leave a message after the tone. Beeeep.'

'The eagle 'as landed,' Trevor whispered into the handset in a cockney accent supposed to disguise his voice, just in case the recorded message was being stored or the phone was tapped. Who knew what technology was up to these days? He wasn't sure who would possibly be interested in listening to a call made from a random public pay-phone in Cape Town, or why anyone would want to track down this particular voicemail message, but he reckoned you could never take too many precautions in a situation like this. Where the cockney accent had come from, he wasn't sure. He also did a pretty good Spanish accent, and quite a decent Irish one, too. Maybe he could have been an actor, he thought, adding it to his growing list of parallel-universe careers, all of which would have saved him his current trauma. 'I repeat,' he muttered in his best East End cockney, 'the eagle 'as landed, guv'nor.'

Trevor hadn't expected the call to go to message, so he hadn't really planned what he was going to say. 'It's all over the internet, mate,' he trailed off, feeling foolish, his voice quavering. 'Our project seems to 'ave gone smoothly. Soooo, I've got my pager wiv me, so you let me know when and where and 'ow you'd like to meet, to make final payment for the, for the … the photo-shoot,' he said. 'Like we agreed, orright? It was you though, innit? Just checking. I mean, I know we said next week, so you're a little early, but … success, yeah? Well, let me know.'

The phone bleeped, indicating that the message recorder had come to an end, whether he was finished speaking or not. And then there was nothing left in his ear but the rush of his heartbeat and the drone of the dialling tone.

Trevor stood on the pavement staring at the cars streaming by, but not really seeing anything. He'd done it. He'd actually done it, and soon his problems would be over. He'd never actually considered what life would be like once the deed had been done. It was surreal. His knees shook with a mixture of nerves and adrenalin and elation and fear and shock and disgust. Relief, too. So many emotions squeezed into one moment, his head was spinning. And he was starving. He could murder a croissant.

THE CO-AUTHORS

'Hey man, Marco, did you hear?'

'Shaun? What?'

'Are you sitting down?'

'No, I'm at the restaurant prepping bok choy. What is it?'

'It's Noakes. You should probably sit down.'

'You're freaking me out. What's going on, Shaun?'

'You haven't seen the news?'

'Jesus Christ, just spit it out! You're scaring me.'

'Noakes is dead.'

'What the fuck are you talking about?'

'The domestic worker found his body in his kitchen last night. He was still alive, but in critical condition. He died in the ambulance on the way to the hospital.'

'No! I can't believe it! What happened?'

'They're not sure. But there's a picture doing the rounds on the internet, one of the neighbours took it on their cell phone at the scene before the ambulance arrived, so it's dark and a bit blurry.'

'Was it a home invasion?'

'They're not sure yet; but they don't think anything was stolen.'

'Wait, what does that even mean? Are you saying that someone might have murdered him, like on purpose?'

'It's possible. Like I said, they're not saying. I can't believe you haven't heard about it yet. Twitter is going nuts. In fact, the entire internet is on fire.'

'I was at the market first thing, and I just got to the restaurant, and it's crazy here,' Marco said. 'They don't know how he died? How is that possible?'

'Well, that's the other thing. They can't do an autopsy to determine cause of death.'

'Why the hell not?'

'Well, this is the insane bit. The latest news is that the ambulance taking him to hospital when he died was hijacked, with the body in it.'

Marco staggered and sat down, still clutching the phone to his ear. 'What?'

'Yup. They don't even know where he is now,' Shaun said.

'Fuck. This is unbelievable. Do you think whoever killed him hijacked the ambulance?'

'To get rid of any evidence before an autopsy was done? Maybe.'

'My head is literally spinning. Have you spoken to Xolisa and Shireen yet?' Marco asked.

'Yeah, I just got off the phone with Shireen, and I'm with Xolisa. They saw it online. It must have happened too late to make it into the morning papers.'

'How are they?'

'Shocked, freaked out, crying.'

'Christ... What do you think this means for us?'

'Sales will probably go up.'

'For fuck's sake, Shaun!'

'What? It's true. That's what happens when a celebrity dies! Michael Jackson sold more albums after his death than he did the entire decade before.'

'I don't think we should compare the Prof to Michael Jackson.'

'Fine, whatever. Listen, one of us is going to have to take over as the public face of this whole enterprise now that he's gone.'

'Jesus, Shaun. His body, wherever it is, is barely cold. How can you even think about something like that at a time like this?'

'Well, someone has to think about it! It's all of our futures at stake here. We can't fart about wringing our hands because one of us is no longer around. Someone needs to take charge, and I, for one, am up for the job.'

'Shaun, please tell me you didn't have anything to do with his death. It wasn't you, was it?'

'What? Wait, you think *I* killed him? Are you out of your freaking mind?'

'No, but I mean, I have to ask. You don't seem particularly thrown by his death, to be honest. And I know how difficult it's been for us, and you especially, to accept that we're just the nameless co-authors behind the scenes, while he's been the one getting more famous by the day. Nobody calls it the Shaun diet, the Marco diet, the Xolisa diet or the Shireen diet: it's the Noakes diet. Everyone knows that hasn't been easy for you to handle, Shaun.'

'That's rich! You've been just as frustrated as me. Plus you've hardly had an easy run with that dead-end, money-pit restaurant of yours. I'm sure it'll get a much-needed boost now with all the press we're about to get. You must have thought at some point that it would do a whole lot better if you had more of a public profile.'

'For the sake of our partnership and our friendship, I'm going to pretend you didn't just say that, Shaun. We should stop this conversation now before one of us says more stuff we might regret. Something traumatic has happened, we're upset, in shock. And we shouldn't be having this kind of conversation over the phone, anyway. You never know who might be listening in.'

There was silence on the other end of the phone for a moment.

'Fine. The police and the press are going to want a statement from each of us. We should get together to figure out what we're going to say,' Shaun spat.

'A statement?'

'Sure, don't be such an idiot! It's a fucking murder, we're his closest business partners, they're going to hang us upside down and give us a good shake, looking for answers to fall out. I'll set up a time, we can Skype with Shireen in Joburg. I'll text you the details,' Shaun said.

'I can't believe this is fucking happening.'

'Oh and Marco…'

'What?'

'Don't talk to the press until we've gotten together and worked out what we're going to say, okay?'

'Jesus, what do you take me for? Of course I won't.'

Marco slammed down the phone, then placed the knife he was clutching down on the counter and breathed deeply. He thought he'd come across as appropriately surprised and horrified, which was important. He didn't want Shaun to know that he already knew about the Prof's death. He'd been practicing his surprised response and his devastated face all morning; it was going to come in handy over the next few weeks, he thought, returning to his bok choy.

THE EX-PUBLISHER

'You're late,' Clive snapped at Frank from behind his stupid face and his stupid tie and his ridiculous glasses.

'I had business to attend to; it won't happen again,' Frank said to his boss, before muttering 'fuck off, you adolescent cunt, or you'll be next,' under his breath as he struggled to pin his name badge to his chest with his left hand.

'Jissus, what happened to your hand?' Clive asked.

'None of your fucking business,' Frank mumbled.

'It's bleeding! Are you okay?' Clive walked towards him from behind the bookstore counter.

'It's nothing,' Frank said, loudly enough for Clive to hear this time, giving up on his name badge and leaving it unpinned and dangling above his shirt pocket.

'You're bleeding all over the place, and your hand looks really swollen. In fact, it's blue. Are you sure you didn't break it?'

'I told you, it's nothing. I punched a wall, that's all,' Frank said.

'What on earth for?'

'Anger, celebration … or maybe I just had an itch.' The sarcasm dripped from Frank's mouth.

'Come to the office, I've got a first-aid kit. We can put a bandage on it,' Clive offered.

'I'm fine,' Frank said. 'Really, I'm better than I've been in ages.'

'Okay, but don't get blood on any of the books,' Clive called after him. 'You bleed on it, you buy it!'

'I promise I won't bleed on your precious books,' Frank said wearily.

'And once you've stopped bleeding, I need you to reorganise African Fiction. That section is a disaster.'

'It's going to take more than a bit of reorganising to fix African Fiction,' Frank mumbled.

'What's that?' Clive asked.

'I said, I'm on my way.'

It was bullshit, Frank thought as he shuffled the books in African Fiction around with his left hand, his right one dangling uselessly by his side, the knuckles throbbing. American bookstores didn't have shelves specifically for American fiction. Bookstores in the UK didn't separate books according to their origin. Fiction was fiction; it didn't matter where it came from. It only mattered if it was any good. South African bookstores had been getting it all wrong for years.

If he was in charge he would … he had to stop and remind himself that he had been in charge once upon a time, not so long ago, and he'd cocked it all up royally. And then his whole life had fallen apart.

He pushed the thought out of his mind and whistled as he worked. He wasn't going to let any of this bullshit ruin his good mood. This was *his* day and he felt great, better than great, in fact. He finally had the revenge he'd been waiting for for two years. Sweet, sweet revenge. The image of that old geezer lying all bloody on the floor would be forever engrained in his brain.

Maybe now that fraudulent Professor would be forgotten. Maybe now that he was dead, people would no longer be bamboozled by his medically irresponsible bullshit. And maybe, just maybe, he would stop being everywhere Frank turned, a constant reminder of his biggest, baddest failure.

Noakes was dead! Nothing was going to get Frank down today, not his shithead boss who was half his age, his dumb-as-a-plank customers, or all those annoying assistants just days out of the womb. He whistled as he finished reorganising African Fiction, then shifted over to Self Help. Books were still his happy place.

He scanned the shelf and shook his head; none of the books were in the right order here either. The *Chicken Soup for the Soul* book needed to be swopped with *How Much Joy Can You Stand?*, which was actually where *If You Had Controlling Parents* should be. He pulled the books off the shelves one by one with his good hand, and then placed them back in alphabetical order.

Frank paused at a book called, *Are You Living or Surviving?* He balanced it on the shelf and paged through it, turning his nose up at the chapters offering tips on improving health, finances and romance. He replaced the book, then revisited *How Much Joy Can You Stand?* by Suzanne Falter-Barns.

'I don't know, Suzanne,' he said to himself, 'right now I'm pretty fucking joyful.'

'Excuse me...' a voice cut in, interrupting his train of thought. 'Do you work here?'

Frank considered shaking his head, but then remembered he was in a great mood, so he nodded.

'Oh goodie,' the middle-aged woman said. 'I'm looking for a nice book, what would you recommend?'

'What are you looking for?' Frank asked. 'Fiction or non-fiction?'

'We're going on holiday, and I have to have something good to read,' the woman said, clutching the pendant on her chest between her fingers and spinning it on its chain. 'Definitely fiction.'

Frank turned to the fiction shelf. 'This is great,' he said as he tugged a new Kate Atkinson novel off the shelf awkwardly with his left hand and handed it to the woman.

She examined the back cover for half a second, then scrunched up her nose and handed it back.

'Too serious,' she said.

Frank fumbled as he replaced the book with his left hand. Then he pointed at the latest Marion Keyes. 'She's great,' he said, not wanting to pick it up with his left hand if she wasn't sure she wanted it – everyone knew Keyes wrote heavy books – literally, not figuratively. 'It's the perfect holiday read, so they say.'

The woman slipped it off the shelf herself and eyed the front cover for a millisecond before replacing it. 'I just don't know,' she said, her voice a kettle-boiling whine. 'You don't have that new *Fifty Shades of Grey* book everyone has been talking about, do you?'

Frank sighed, led her wordlessly to the front of the store, and handed her the latest spin on the bestseller. A million copies sold in its first week. The injustice of it threatened to ruin his good mood for a second.

The woman took the book from him without thanking him and made her way to the till. Frank shook off the encounter and started whistling again as he followed her.

'Hey,' Siya greeted him, or maybe it was Mark, or Phil, or Khanya, or who cared? The myriad revolving-door university students who part-timed alongside him in the bookstore were all the same. They all seemed impossibly young, and Frank couldn't be arsed to remember their names. It wasn't like he was going to hang out and discuss the latest Vladislavić with any of them.

As a forty-six-year-old man working as a sales assistant in a massive chain bookstore, he knew he stood out like erotica in the kiddies section, and he knew the other staff all talked about him behind his back, but he couldn't give a fuck. Especially today: today, he couldn't even give two fucks.

'You're in a good mood,' the stripling assistant commented.

Frank carried on whistling.

'I haven't seen you in a good mood since … well come to think of it, I don't think I've ever seen you in a good mood,' the boy said.

'Yeah? Well, first time for everything,' Frank said.

'Did you see the news about that Banting guy?' the kid asked.

'I heard.' Frank gave a small self-satisfied smile.

'It's crazy, right?'

'Wild.'

'Just awful!' the perky girl assistant with the short dreadlocks chimed in.

'Too terrible,' Frank added, unable to stop his small smile developing into a wide grin.

'I wonder who offed the poor guy?' the boy said.

'It was me,' Frank said, straight-faced, looking the kid right in the eyes.

The boy looked at him with surprise, and then burst out laughing.

Frank continued to stare at him, unwavering, willing the boy to challenge him.

'Ha, good one, Frank,' the boy said, slapping him on the shoulder.

Another woman entered the store and made a beeline for the tills. She had dirty-blonde hair that reminded Frank of his wife – or rather, his ex-wife, even though this woman was much heavier than Sylvie had been when they finally divorced. This customer carried her weight in her belly and her hips, just like Sylvie had. Her jeans stretched mercilessly at the seams.

Frank wondered where his ex-wife was right this second. She was probably getting ready for her gym session. After her workout, she'd head off for a spot of lunch, something healthy no doubt. No more junk for her. Then she would fetch Chloe from school and take her to ballet class, and then she'd probably go fuck her gym-instructor boyfriend for an hour in the fucking house Frank had paid for. She was looking incredible these days, but then she had really put in a lot of effort. Fuck, he hated her and her now perfect tight ass and incredible divorce-settlement-shop-bought tits. Fuck her.

'Hi,' the woman said. 'I'm looking for that Banting book. Do you have it?'

'I think we've sold out,' the boy told her apologetically. 'We've got more coming in on order.'

Frank whipped his head around. 'What!' he yelled.

'Sold out again?' the perky girl piped up. 'Sheesh, that's like the hundredth time this year, dude.' She had a ring in her nose, like a bull.

'Yup, we've had a major run on them this morning, because of the news of the Prof's death, I guess. We've already sold, like, twelve or fifteen copies at least, and we've been open less than an hour.'

'Oh, you've got to be fucking shitting me!' Frank said.

'Yup. Amazing what a little death will do for sales,' the boy said as he restacked the adult colouring-in books on the counter. Another stupid craze that made Frank want to shoot himself in the head. 'I called some of our other branches. They've sold out everywhere: Canal Walk, the Waterfront, even the airport.'

'Jesus!' Frank bellowed. 'That's it. I can't do this anymore.' He stepped out from behind the till counter.

'Where are you going?' the kid looked confused.

'I need a drink,' Frank said.

'But it's not even ten yet,' pointed out bullring nose.

'You know Clive will fire you if you walk out in the middle of a shift, hey?' the boy called out after him.

'Kid, it won't be the first job I've been fired from,' Frank announced. As he walked towards the door of the store, he swiped his hand across the main display table, knocking the neatly stacked piles of bestsellers and new arrivals onto the floor with a clatter. He paused, turned, and punched the life-sized cardboard cutout of Tim Noakes in the face. He shouted as pain shot through his damaged fist, and up his arm. He hopped up and down, swearing and nursing his hand for a moment, then he dropped his hurt arm and continued punching the cutout with his left hand, over and over again, until it collapsed. Then he stamped all over it, bent and tore at the head, screaming, 'Fuck you, fuck you, fuck you!' The young assistants and the customers stood inside the doorway watching him, their mouths gaping.

At last Frank levered himself upright and stomped off through the mall.

'It's fine, I'm leaving, I'm leaving!' he shouted, as he passed a security guard walking towards the commotion, speaking into his radio. 'I need a drink anyway.'

THE HIJACKERS

'Hold him up on your side,' Thabo hissed.

'I am holding him up on my side,' Papsak snapped back. 'You hold him up on your side, wena!'

The woman in the seat in front of them turned and stared.

'Molo, Mama,' Thabo said, smiling at her politely. She scowled at them, then heaved herself forward again.

The second she wasn't looking at them, Thabo glared at Papsak, then adjusted the beanie and the oversized sunglasses, which had started slipping off the dead man's face.

'What's wrong with Umlungu?' the taxi driver shouted over his shoulder.

Papsak and Thabo eyed each other nervously.

'Too much shisa nyama,' Thabo said.

'He's my uncle,' Papsak said.

Thabo gave Papsak a filthy look and tried to tell him to shut up telepathically.

The driver turned in his seat to side-eye Papsak, and his taxi swayed dangerously into the next lane, making the mama shout at him.

Papsak adjusted the sunglasses, which were slipping down the dead man's face once again.

'This mlungu? Your uncle?' asked the driver, facing forward.

'Yes. He's married to my mother's sister,' Papsak explained, shrugging at Thabo.

'Hawu!' exclaimed the mama, clicking her tongue.

'It's his birthday,' Thabo said. 'We just came from his party. Too much phuza. We're taking him home so he can sober up before he goes home to my aunt, otherwise she will kill him.'

'And us,' Papsak added.

The taxi driver eyed them warily through the rearview mirror.

'For an extra ten, can you drop us outside Lefty's shebeen?' Thabo asked.

The taxi driver swerved into the other lane without indicating, and the corpse's head bobbed sideways, landing on Papsak's shoulder. Papsak patted him on the beanie. 'Happy birthday, Uncle Mlungu.'

THE CO-AUTHORS

'Thank you for taking the time to chat to me over the phone, Mr Cannata. Particularly during what must be a difficult time of mourning for you. I won't keep you long, I only have a few questions to help fill in some background for the story we'll be running on Sunday.'

Marco had already forgotten the journalist's name. 'Please, call me Marco. I'm happy to help, if you think it will shed some light on this terrible tragedy.'

'So would you say you were close to Professor Noakes, Mr Ca— Marco?'

'Of course we were close; I mean, we've written books together. He's been like a father to me. He even helped me start my restaurant, the Banting Bistro, which is on Kloof Street in Cape Town.'

'And how did you two meet originally?'

'Umm, it all started back in 2012 when Prof, that's what I always call ... I mean, called him, got in touch with me. He told me he had an idea for a groundbreaking book on nutrition, and he was looking for a talented chef to co-author it with him. At the time I was actually about to enter *MasterChef South Africa*. I'd made it through all the first rounds of interviews. But Prof ... sorry, give me a moment...' (deep breath) 'when the Prof told me about his journey, and he took me through some of his early research, it all made sense to me, and I could see how important his project was. So I put aside my lifelong dream of going on *MasterChef* and agreed to work on the book with him. Then he brought in the other three after that. Partnering with the Prof has easily been one of the best decisions I've ever made.'

'I'm sure. After all, the book has sold very well, hasn't it? Do you have any idea who would want to hurt Professor Noakes?' the journalist prodded.

'God, no. What an incredible, inspirational man. Of course, there are a lot of crazies out there; just look at his Twitter feed. But look at how many lives we've changed for the better with this book. And now I'm hoping to continue the journey in his memory, with a new secret project I've been very busy with for the last six months, which I can't talk about yet. And of course I also extend his legacy through my restaurant, the Banting Bistro, in Kloof Street. I've even decided to name a dish after him. Noakes Zoodles: courgette noodles with basil pesto and garlic, for just forty-seven rand ninety-five. Will you include that in the piece?'

'I can try to put that in, but my editor will probably zap it. We always have space issues.'

'Thanks, if you could see what you can do, I'd appreciate the exposure.'

'Marco, there has been some talk of a rift between you and your co-authors,' the journo started smoothly.

'What? Who said that?'

'I'm sure it's all just baseless rumours, you know how these things go, but of course I have to follow up on them.'

'Sure, but I don't know of any rift.'

'So there's been no frustration or unhappiness between the four of you? Over how little publicity you've all gotten in comparison with Professor Noakes, let's say?'

'That's ridiculous! Did Shaun say that? That might be how my co-authors feel, but I can only speak for myself, and I've never been happier. In fact, I've been so busy setting up my restaurant, the Banting Bistro, in Kloof Street, which is open daily for breakfast, lunch and dinner, that I've been grateful to the Prof for taking the lead on this project as far as publicity is concerned. He saved my bacon, so to speak.'

'Sure, that makes sense. And Marco, what about the rumours concerning your dissatisfaction with your author photographs?'

'What rumours? What dissatisfaction?' Marco asked.

'Well, it can't have passed you by that you don't really ... how can I put this ... the author photograph on the book, and the ones the press have in circulation, they don't look very much like you in real life, do they? There seems to have been some ... well, to be frank, a lot of air-brushing. And the way they've positioned you, it's like half of you has been cropped out of the shot, don't you think? You can't have been happy about that.'

Cheeky bastard. 'Look, I'm a chef, not a photographer or a model,' Marco said through gritted teeth. 'I came up with every single recipe in that book, from scratch. That's what I do. How our publisher chooses to market it is entirely up to them. I don't get involved in that side of the business, it's not my concern or area of expertise.'

'Okay, so to be clear: you've never had *any* problems with *any* of your co-authors, and you're a hundred per cent happy with your author photographs?' the journalist prodded.

'Look, this is a creative endeavour we're involved in, and when there's collaboration of this kind, and a number of different egos involved, some compromise is always going to be necessary. But we've never fallen out over anything. And anyway, I really don't see what this has got to do with the Prof's death. Quite honestly, I think it's insensitive of you to ask these sorts of questions when we're all going through something this traumatic.'

'Absolutely, Mr Cannata, and I am really sorry for your loss. Thank you for your time,' the journalist said.

'Wouldn't you rather talk a bit about the concept behind the book, or some of my recipes, maybe? Like which was the Prof's favourite? And which ones I serve in my restaurant, the Banting Bistro? Anything like that?'

'Not to worry, your co-author already gave me quite a bit of background info. I've pretty much got everything I need for now.'

'You spoke to Shaun?' Marco asked, clenching his jaw. 'When?'

'I just got off the phone with him; he gave me a lot of really great background info. I've got your number, so I'll be sure to get in touch if I need anything else. Thanks for your time.' The phone went dead.

The black-and-red pencil Marco was holding between his fingers snapped in half.

THE FANS

THE BANTING FOR LIFE FACEBOOK PAGE

Nicky Page
Hi, new banter here. Which list are sprouts on? Good, bad or ugly?
Like 24

Chantal Duining Good!
Like 13

John Combrink Ugh
Like 0

Nicky Page Thank you **Chantal Duining**
Like 1

John Combrink
This is what annoys me so much about this fad; red lists, green lists, orange lists, it's all nonsense. The trick to health and successful weight loss is to eat everything in moderation. It's a terrible idea to deprive your body of an entire food group. Can't you people see how foolish this concept is, or are you all just sheep who can't think for yourselves? It's irresponsible and downright untenable for Noakes, as a member of the medical profession, to encourage this kind of anti-nutrition just to make a buck. He's become a laughing-stock. Wrap anything in bacon and you'll sell a truckload of it!
He should be ashamed of himself; we have zero research on the effects this kind of exclusionary diet will have on generations to come.
Although I don't know why I'm here trying to talk all you idiots out of Banting. I'm a medical practitioner, more business for me down the line, when you all get kidney stones or heart disease and then you come running to me. Consider yourselves warned.
Like 2
View 2973 more comments

THE WIDOW

Maureen scheduled the seven meal-plan orders that had already come flying into her inbox via direct message that morning (seven more than she'd had in the last three weeks). Then she boiled the kettle and took a cup of tea (with cream) back to the dining-room table, which she liked to think of as Facebook Headquarters.

Some months ago she'd moved the chairs from one side of the dining-room table into the spare room, then she'd pushed the table up against the wall. It was now permanently covered in all her papers, books and notes. There was also a large pinboard, which she'd propped on the table and leaned against the dining-room wall.

The pinboard had been a great purchase; she'd picked it up at CNA shortly after she'd started posting, but now she was starting to run out of space, as well as pins. The thought that she might have to buy another pinboard excited her. Or maybe she would tile the entire one wall of the dining room with cork, it's not like she threw dinner parties anymore.

The board was carefully divided into columns, using packaging string. Each column contained one of her personas, their user name and passwords for their respective Facebook and email accounts, as well as some of their basic vital statistics, including height, hair colour and other outstanding features. It also contained scribbled notes that covered some of their individual quirks (for example, in Herman's column was a small scrap of paper with 'he prefers beer to spirits' on it), as well as the times and dates of each persona's individual postings on the Banting for Life Facebook page, and so on. There was also a carefully logged chart plotting each persona's weight loss in detail. It was Maureen's master plan, and it was essential in helping her keep all her stories straight.

Her habit of posting as other personas had all started with Herman. Once her own weight loss had slowed and ultimately plateaued at her goal weight, she found she had less and less reason to post on the group's page, and the responses to her posts started to dwindle too. She still commented on other people's posts, but it wasn't the same. She missed the kick of adrenalin she got at seeing that dozens of people had liked one of her comments, then logging in a few hours later to see that the likes had gone up into the hundreds. The day she had posted her most dramatic before-and-after photographs, her likes had rocketed into the thousands. It made her bubble with excitement just to remember it. Not to mention the hundreds of comments, thumbs-up stickers, friend requests and votes of confidence she regularly received as a result of the page.

It was then that she'd realised something had been missing from her life since Gus had died. For the first time, she hadn't felt the cold ache of loneliness. She finally had the network of support she'd been craving; perhaps she could even consider all these new internet voices her friends?

After that, it wasn't a huge leap for her to come up with the idea of starting all over again, and that was when she invented Herman. All she had to do was come up with a name and a persona for him; in her mind, he was a simplified version of Gus. She'd lived with him for nearly forty years: she knew him inside and out and all around. Plus, recreating him on a Facebook page made her feel more connected to him, as if he was still there, Banting right alongside her.

Creating a Facebook profile for Herman/Gus was easy-peasy. Once she'd figured out Facebook, she had discovered that all you needed to create a new profile was an email address, which was a piece of (wheat-free) cake, thanks to Gmail, Yahoo and Hotmail.

It was tricky remembering all the different passwords and user log-ins, but that's what the pinboard was for, stabbed with dozens of notes.

Another hard part had been coming up with names for all her new personas. Even though her first one was Gus inside and out, right down to his stubborn refusal to try even one tiny mouthful of rocket, despite how she cooked it or tried to disguise it in spinach, she didn't want to call him Gus. It felt too close to the bone. He also couldn't be named after anyone she already knew or had been at school with. What if they were on Facebook and stumbled across their namesake and saw her commenting on and liking their posts, and put two and two together? No, it was too risky.

At first she was concerned that whatever names she came up with sounded contrived. She considered using the name of a character from whatever book she was reading at the time, but who on earth was called Heathcliff these days? Eventually, she settled on Herman De Laat for her Gus character.

Some months later, when 'Herman' started to bore and even annoy her (as Gus often had in real life), and when interest in him on the page started to wane (especially after he'd admitted to cheating with dried fruit, garnering a number of passive-aggressive comments and ranty lectures), Maureen had created her second persona, Lydia Steenberg.

Here Maureen had simply cobbled together the names of two people she'd been at school with: the first name of a girl in her class she had always envied, together with the surname of a boy she'd fancied. Lydia, a sweet young blonde, was the kind of woman Maureen thought she might be close friends with herself, if she were twenty or thirty years younger.

Another trick she discovered was to find or create friends for these people so that if anyone followed them, they would appear to be legitimate human beings. It was an elaborate process that took time and required a lot of 'friending' of strangers on Facebook. But time was the one thing Maureen had plenty of – long days stretching ahead of her with nothing much to fill them. And it turned out there were lots of other people out there who also had time on their hands, and no problems accepting a friend request from a perfect stranger with no mutual friends, or any other visible connections, other than a shared favourite recipe, or both enjoying the same sort of music.

A few months after Lydia, came Sizwe Madonda, who was Maureen's most ambitious and challenging persona yet. She decided to really push herself out of her comfort zone.

Sizwe was a thirty-seven-year-old black man who liked his pap and beer. He was going through a divorce, and learning to cook for himself, which he was finding a great challenge. Sizwe would burn water if you gave him half a chance. Maureen scanned her notes on Sizwe, which were tacked to the pinboard. He was a Kaizer Chiefs supporter who was coming along nicely weight-wise, slowly inching closer to his goal every month. Coming up with these characters and figuring out their lives was a little like writing a book, Maureen imagined. And she'd always wanted to do that.

It was shortly after Maureen had created Sizwe that she came up with the idea of developing and selling Banting meal plans to other members of the group. All self-help books said that the most successful people were those who turned their hobbies into their jobs, so why not her? She'd seen someone else doing it on the Banting for Life page, offering professional LCHF meal plans for cash. How hard could it be? She loved cooking and experimenting in the kitchen, and she was an ardent Banting convert who'd read the book four times. Plus, she already had three dedicated customers who would be happy to give her little meal plans free advertising on the Banting for Life Facebook Page. Good old Herman, Lydia and Sizwe would be her first clients.

Unfortunately the meal plan business hadn't taken off as well as Maureen had hoped, but now that she could at last claim that her meal plans were ENDORSED by the Professor himself, she had a feeling they were going to be a huge success.

Maureen logged out of Facebook as herself and logged back in as Lydia Steenberg. Lydia had six new notifications, and one new direct message. Maureen scrolled through the notifications first – most of them were responses to threads she had followed on the Banting for Life page. But one notification was from Facebook, informing Lydia that one of her randomly friended 'friends', Simone Kunderman, had a birthday.

'Happy birthday, have a great day,' Lydia quickly tapped out on the stranger's wall.

Within seconds, Simone had acknowledged the message by liking it. Maureen wondered what Simone thought. Perhaps she thought Lydia was an old school friend who had a different surname now, or a work colleague she didn't remember, but was too polite to question the source of their friendship. Maureen found it remarkable how little visual evidence one needed to create an entire human being online, one with a birthday, a history, friends and family, likes and dislikes.

When she'd first created Lydia, Maureen had surfed Google images for pictures that could believably make up Lydia's life. She was careful to choose obscure photographs of various young, overweight blonde women, all shot from behind or a bit blurry to protect her theft of their identities, but still similar enough to seem legitimate. Maureen also decided that Lydia had a cat named Ginger Mary, a generic-looking feline who was obsessed with dragging Lydia's imaginary neighbours' socks off their washing line into Lydia's imaginary house. The imaginary Ginger Mary liked sleeping in Lydia's imaginary laundry basket on top of Lydia's imaginary clean clothes. She might not exist, but Lydia Steenberg was as vivid in Maureen's mind as if she were her daughter or next-door neighbour.

Maureen checked her plan on the pinboard, and then uploaded a new photograph of a ginger cat to Lydia's profile, right on schedule. Maybe because in her mind they were such great friends, Maureen had taken things with Lydia further than she ever had with Herman or Sizwe. She'd even chosen a couple of pleasing hobbies for the young woman. She decided that Lydia would enjoy reading local fiction and knitting, and regularly posted pictures of the books she was busy reading, the kinds of books Maureen imagined a girl like her would like – none of that *Fifty Shades* nonsense.

Lydia was an only child, Maureen had decided, with a relatively low-pressure job in Human Resources at a large computer company, and she sometimes went for a drink after work with a small group of girlfriends she'd had since school, and one or two she'd met later at college or in the workplace.

When Maureen first started posting as Lydia in the Banting group, the twenty-seven-year-old blonde needed to lose about twenty-five kilos. Her journey hadn't been an easy one, on purpose. Because, Maureen felt, everybody loved an underdog.

Poor Lydia had really struggled to lose weight at first. She'd even put on five kilos in her first few months of Banting, and had become very despondent about the whole thing. If it hadn't been for the communal strength and encouragement of the group (and cutting down on her imaginary dairy and in-between meal snacks), she would have most certainly given up.

Maureen thought it was an inspired idea to present a different kind of Banting journey. Herman had been almost immediately successful with his efforts at losing weight (as Maureen herself had been). So this was something different for her. And the fans loved it. Their encouragement even buoyed up Maureen herself, especially whenever she was considering a sneaky rusk with her bullet-proof coffee.

Maureen's most popular comment ever came a few weeks after Lydia had first started Banting, when she'd posted two silly before-and-after photos of Ginger Mary that made the cat look like she'd lost a couple of feline kilos. Over seven hundred likes, one hundred and fifty-seven shares, and two hundred and twenty comments and counting. It was as if Maureen had gone viral.

Now, Lydia was really close to reaching her goal weight, thanks to Banting and Maureen's Marvellous Tim Noakes ENDORSED Meal Plans. Just the other day, Maureen had replaced Lydia's blurry, fat-from-behind profile picture with another side-on, generic picture of a pretty blonde girl she'd found buried somewhere on Google. And Lydia had posted that she was now the gorgeous, sexy, confident girl she had always wanted to be, thanks to Maureen's Marvellous Tim Noakes ENDORSED Meal Plans.

Maureen clicked through to Lydia's messages, curious and slightly nervous; who could possibly be writing to an imaginary human being?

BENJAMIN

Benjamin Di Rosi Hi Lydia, you don't know me from a bar of soap, and I hope you don't think it's too forward of me to friend you like this on Facebook and private message you so completely out of the blue? But for the last few weeks I've really wanted to write to tell you how much your progress and your posts on the Banting for Life Page have inspired me. I hope you don't mind me getting in touch? I also couldn't help noticing that you've been using Maureen's Marvellous Meal Plans. Which are apparently endorsed by Professor Noakes himself (RIP). I wanted to ask how those are working for you, as I'm considering signing up. As a single man, I struggle to come up with ideas of new things to make, and a ready-made meal plan feels like the perfect solution. I hope to hear back from you.

> Lydia Steenberg Hello Benjamin. Thank you for your kind words. I'm so glad you friended me and wrote. Banting has been one of the best things that has ever happened to me, and this group has been such amazing support. So if there's ever any opportunity to share that support, then that's my greatest pleasure. I must tell you, I absolutely LOVE Maureen's ENDORSED by Prof Noakes (RIP, his death is just too sad for words) Marvellous Meal Plans. I find they work really well for me and I can honestly HIGHLY recommend them. You should totally do it. And I know what you mean about being single, and struggling to find menu ideas, I have the exact same problem.

Benjamin Di Rosi How great of you to write back so quickly. I wasn't really expecting a response, so you made my day. I find it hard to believe that a woman as beautiful as you could be single. Believe it or not, I coincidentally started Banting at around about the same time as you, so I've been really grateful to be able to follow your journey alongside my own. Whenever I feel like I'm struggling or feel tempted to reach for what I like to call 'contraband', I think about the incredible success and the immense will to succeed that you and so many other people in the group have shown, and it always keeps me on the straight and narrow. I'm definitely going to look into getting in touch with Maureen about her meal plans, since you speak so highly of them. Perhaps we could share some notes and information about how we are doing?

> Lydia Steenberg Oh how lovely of you to say that thing about being inspired by my journey. It hasn't been easy, but I'm so glad I'm doing it. Sometimes I think everyone on that group makes it look easier than it really is. I can tell you honestly that I also have my run-ins with contraband. Sometimes I just say what the heck, and treat myself. We're only human after all. I was just looking at your profile (blush – I wasn't Facebook stalking you, I promise) and it looks like you've done amazingly well. How much have you lost in total so far? And yes, I'd love to swop notes with you.

Benjamin Di Rosi Ah, now it's my turn to blush. Yes, I've had incredible results. I've lost over 20 kilos since I started, I'm pleased to say.

> Lydia Steenberg Wow, that's fantastic! Well done you! But how come you haven't posted about it on the page? I'm sure I would have seen and congratulated you if you had.

Benjamin Di Rosi I guess I'm kind of shy. I prefer to watch and be inspired by everyone on the page, like youAkdfjlakifhfhfhf fkjfkfj kjfa kdajf akdjf alfdka f

I'm SO sorry, that wasn't me. My crazy cat just walked right across my keyboard!

> Lydia Steenberg Ha ha ha I wondered what happened there. I have a cat too, Ginger Mary. No surprises, she's a ginger. What's your cat's name?

Benjamin Di Rosi Yes I've seen pictures of your Ginger Mary on your profile on Facebook (I also wasn't stalking you, I swear!) Those before and after pics were hilarious!! My cat's name is Silas. He loves my keyboard. He especially likes walking across it when I'm working or typing, and sometimes, mostly when I'm working on something especially important, he likes to lie across it, as if he owns it. It's his party trick, to get my attention. I'd better go and feed him before he finds something else to destroy. But I'm looking forward to chatting to you again if you're keen?

Lydia Steenberg Sometimes I think we're our cat's pets, instead of the other way around.

Benjamin Di Rosi So true ☺ Chat soon.

Lydia Steenberg Bye, Benjamin. Bye, Silas.

'You okay?'

The man in Frank's peripheral vision seemed chatty, and Frank wasn't in the mood for chatty, so he ignored him. He didn't come to this bar to be sociable – he came to drink and to forget. Well, to drink to forget.

'Hey buddy,' the man said again, a little louder.

Frank went on pretending he hadn't heard him.

'Hey man, you know your hand's bleeding all over the bar, right?' The guy shifted from his barstool to the barstool beside Frank's.

'It's nothing,' Frank murmured, not making eye-contact in an effort to make it clear that he wasn't in the mood for small talk with an annoyingly hairy stranger who smelled like pickled onions.

'It doesn't look like nothing. It looks like you've been in a hell of a fight. I'd hate to see what the other guy looks like,' said the man cheerily. 'So, what happened to you?'

At last Frank swivelled in his seat to face the man. 'You know when you're involved in something really big that happens, and you think it's going to change your life completely, but it doesn't, and your life stays just as shit as it was before that big thing happened? But the problem is that you were counting on that big thing to change your life and make it better, but in reality, nothing changes, in fact that big thing just ends up exacerbating the problem and making everything worse.'

'Er, I think so.'

'Well, that,' said Frank, swivelling back to face the bar.

'So what did you do to your hand?' the man persisted.

'You ask a lot of questions for a stranger in a bar,' Frank spat. 'What are you, the FB-fucking-I?'

'Sorreeee! Excuse me for living,' the man said. 'But your hand's bleeding all over the bar and there's not much else going on around here, so it made me curious. No offence,' he added, waving at the barman. 'Want another?' he asked Frank.

Frank nodded. Who was he to turn down a free drink? In fact, who was he to turn down a free anything?

'I punched something,' Frank said, by way of payment for his drink, which was being poured by an uninterested barman. Daytime barmen were always uninterested. They'd either seen too much, or they'd seen it all.

'Is the thing you punched animate or inanimate? Or previously animate and now inanimate?' the man asked.

'It was a wall, okay? Are you happy now? A brick wall! Anything else? My blood type maybe? Where I buy my socks? Boxers or briefs? My ID number? Shoe size?' Frank shouted.

'Well, there's no need to be an arsehole about it!' the man huffed before shifting back to his original seat.

'Good riddance,' muttered Frank, downing his drink in one shot, then nodding at the barman to fill his glass once again.

THE HIJACKERS

'How much do you want for the gusheshe, Lefty?' Thabo asked.

'The price has never changed, magents,' Lefty said, watching them through one eye, working at his teeth with a toothpick. 'In fact, for you two moegoes, it might even go up.'

'Ama-Trevor-Noah,' Thabo said. 'How about twelve grand, special price?'

'That's not the price. The price is twenty grand, I told you,' Lefty said, the eyebrow above the scar where his left eye used to be quivering with annoyance.

Rumour had it that he'd either lost his eye in Pollsmoor, or playing darts with a blind man, depending who you asked about it.

'Twenty grand for that skorokoro?' Thabo feigned indignation. 'It's not worth more than ten, and you know it. It's barely driving.'

'Then be my guest and don't buy it,' Lefty said. 'Nobody is begging you. And that's not a skorokoro, it's a classic car. And if you can't see that, you don't deserve to drive such a fine piece of machinery.'

'Oh please, it's from before the struggle. It's got over two hundred thousand on the clock, easy,' Papsak chimed in.

Lefty shook his head, leaning against the bar counter and continuing to pick his teeth.

Thabo and Papsak exchanged panicked glances.

'Okay, look Lefty, we're not messing you around. We are honest, legit buyers. Look here, we've got fourteen grand, cash,' Thabo said, fishing his wad out of his pocket and nudging Papsak, who rifled around in his own pocket and got out his share. Thabo grabbed Papsak's cash, and held just about every cent they had out to the one-eyed shebeen owner.

Lefty narrowed his good eye, the lines on his forehead furrowing in pockmarked skin. 'Magents must either be deaf or stupid,' he said. 'What part of twenty grand don't you understand?'

'What if we throw in Uncle Mlungu?' Papsak suggested, pointing to a table across the empty shebeen, where the body was sitting, propped up against the corner in his sunglasses, his beanie pulled down low.

'What am I supposed to do with a passed-out white man?' Lefty asked.

'He's not passed out,' Papsak whispered, and Thabo smacked him on the arm.

'What? Stop hitting me!' Papsak shouted, aggrieved. 'He's going to find out soon enough. It's not like we can keep it a secret forever.'

Lefty came out from behind the bar counter and walked slowly towards the occupied table. He turned on the house lights, then leaned in close to the dead mlungu.

'What am I supposed to do with him?' Lefty asked as he straightened and turned back to the two hijackers.

'I don't know,' Papsak said. 'We thought maybe you would want to take him off our hands. You could sell him. Maybe for muti or something.'

Lefty leaned over the mlungu again, and lifted the dead man's sunglasses, flinching at the dried blood and black and blue bruises on the dead man's face. 'Wait, what have you two done now? Is this that famous professor who's in the news now?' Lefty said. 'That professor who's making everyone stop eating bread?'

Thabo and Papsak looked at Uncle Mlungu, then each other. They both shrugged.

'I'm half-blind, and even I can see who it is,' Lefty added.

'How do you know?' Papsak asked.

'Because I'm not a complete ignoramus, I read *Die Son*!' Lefty said. 'It's been all over the news this morning. He was attacked last night, he died in the ambulance, and then some guys hijacked the ambulance. Was that you two rubbishes?'

'Yes,' Papsak said.

'No,' Thabo said, at exactly the same time. Then he smacked Papsak on the arm again.

'Where did you jack the ambulance?' Lefty asked.

'Salt River,' Papsak said.

Lefty whistled slowly, working the toothpick between his lips as he thought for a moment.

'I'll give you moegoes the gusheshe for fourteen, on one condition,' Lefty said.

'What?'

'The two of you get out of here fast and take your new friend with you, and don't ever come back. That body is as hot as Nando's. Every cop in South Africa is looking for it, and I've got enough problems.'

THE FANS

THE BANTING FOR LIFE FACEBOOK PAGE

Dolly Leydt
Hello friendly Banting for Life fans and people. So, my husband and children are all slim thank goodness. But it hasn't been as easy for me. I've always battled to keep the weight off and I think I've been fat my entire life. I have been too scared to do it for ages, but I finally plucked up the courage and I stood on the scale today for the first time in years, to mark the beginning of my Real Meal Revolution journey. I'm too shy to put up a picture of myself, but I weigh 152.6kg, so I know its time for me to do something about it. But I reeaaaalllyyyy need some help and advice and a lot of encouragement from everywhere and anywhere!!! Please. Thank you.
Like 46

Fayrooz Saaiman Dolly you can do this. Today is the first day of the rest of your life. Have you researched the lchf (low carb high fat) lifestyle at all?? and also maybe spoken to your doctor about it to get some help and advise. But I suggest you find a banting friendly doctor. My old doctor told me I shouldn't do it, until I eventually found a new banting friendly doctor here in East London, Doctor Adenauer and he has been great, I've lost 15 kilos and am down to my target weight. It will be hard, but once you get going you will realise it's the best way to eat. What helped for me is to always remember that it's not a deit, it's a way of life
Like 36

Zuki Kwela just cut out all your sugar and also all the carbs from your diet, simple, simple, simple.
Like 21

Barry Sinker Wow good luck Dolly, behind you all the way. But pretty impressive cos most scales only go up to 150 kilos, where did you find that one you are using? (I'm not asking for me, I weigh 82) Did you use an industrial scale or something?
Like 4

Louise Commerford Dolly, my stating weight was 146kg and I lost 52kg in a year and have not gained it back in almost two years. My hubby says I'm half the woman I used to be ☺ - but I have managed to stay with it, it just takes a bit of planning. If I can do it, you can do it too. Im thinking of you.
Like 26

Maureen Ewehout Hi Dolly, congratulations on your brave adventure. It will feel overwhelming at first, but as you learn more and start to shed those pesky kilos, I think you will be so glad you took this first step. Speaking of first steps, if you're looking for any help, I sell a series of Marvellous Meal Plans that have actually been ENDORSED by the late, great Professor Tim Noakes (may he rest in peace). He was my idol, and we worked together very closely to create these specific meal plans, specially designed to help people navigate their way through this journey. Please direct message me if I can help you in any way. And good luck. You can do it.
Like 9

Sue-anne Deeb Dolly, here we all are supporting each other! Push through You can do it! #skinnysoon I will pray for you.
Like 21

Sizwe Madonda Eish, eita sister Dolly! Good luck. I've been using Maureen's ENDORSED meal plans and they worked for me. You can do it, yebo gogo!
Like 13

Wilma Du Toit Dearest Dolly, if you ask me, there is really only one way to diet and that is using the Be-Slim Programme. It's the healthiest way to lose so much weight using a series of delicious shakes and supplements. And the best part of it is that theres no food in the Be-Slim programme that is such a big health risk for heart attacks.
Like 2

Jessa Levigne Well done for being so brave. You can do this if you pretend it's just like rehab and take it one day at a time. Same like AA, the programme really works if you work it.
Like 17

Jordan Sandak Hey **Wilma Du Toit**, you know Be-Slim isn't what we do here, hey? Not quite sure why you are coming here and recommending it to this poor woman who is obviously trying to be brave and start her Banting journey. Do you work for the Be-Slim people maybe??? I hope they pay you a lot. I think the admins should kick you out this group Wilma!!!!
Like 26

Sallique Spuy Dolly, I suggest you check to see if maybe you have some underlining issues that are making your weight be so on the heavy side for all this years. Banting has worked for me. Banting for life!
Like 7

Lydia Steenberg Like **Sizwe Madonda** I've also been using **Maureen Ewehout**'s Marvellous Tim Noakes ENDORSED meal plans and they have really done the trick for me too. Dolly one day you will look back and you'll be so glad that you started TODAY
Like 19

Glenda Adshade Wilma this is none of that stupid Be-Slim nonsense. I don't know where you're even coming from. Banting isn't a diet, not even close! There are no stupid shakes or supplements you have to drink, or pills you have to take. You don't even have to weigh all your food before you eat it. The secret is to eat healthy, REAL food. No sugar, no carbs, stay away from anything that is fake or processed for success.
Like 19

Cornelius Newton Wilma seker dis meer Be nie so Slim nie, as Be-Slim!
See Translation
Like 15

Fran Schenk Wilma Be-Slim didn't work for me and those shakes tasted yuk! Banting food tastes like real food. It's a lot healthyer for you. It's also so much easier to carry on doing as a lifestile over a long period of time!
Like 29

Greg Wright You're all so stupid and gullible, I bet Noakes died from a heart attack from all that lard he's been peddling, and the Real Meal Revolution people are just trying to cover up his death by saying it was a murder to protect themselves and their bottom lines.
Like 3

Jade Van Der Merwe Begin nou om te Bant en jy kan rerig jou kos geniet veel meer as met 'n ander program soos Be-Slim of watookal. Jy kannie bacon eet in die Be-Slim program, daar is geen bacon shake, last time I looked!!!
See Translation
Like 86

Zakes Kekana Just ignore all the haters! They're just jealous and ignorant! You have the best spirit, Dolly. I can feel it and see it in your post. Don't let the fuckers get you down. I am #behindyoualltheway
Like 72
View 567 more comments

THE WIDOW

Wednesday 12:54pm

Maureen's newest persona, Dolly, had surpassed all of her wildest dreams. In just twenty minutes, she'd received the most enthusiastic encouragement and had even inadvertently started a bit of an argument, thanks to that odd Be-Slim woman, who had either landed on the wrong page by accident, or had some kind of death wish.

Maureen was particularly thrilled with Dolly's success in light of the timing. She'd ummed and ahhed over whether to create a new persona at a time when all anyone on the Banting for Life page could talk about was the poor Prof's murder, but Maureen had ultimately decided to give it a bash and see how it turned out. She thought (and she was right) that it would provide people with a welcome distraction from their grief. People needed the release; they needed her.

The club members always liked the beginners. Maybe it was because each new individual who joined their ranks gave their cause legitimacy. And provided added proof that they'd made the right decision changing their lifestyles so drastically. As more fans joined, it made them feel less foolish about following what might just be a fad so religiously. The cultish nature of the group hadn't entirely bypassed Maureen.

Dolly would have some real challenges to face, Maureen thought, as she scribbled some notes. Perhaps Dolly should ask the members some questions about various foods, learning which lists they were on, and she could throw in a hot topic, drop in the name of a contentious product like aspartame or xylitol.

Maybe Dolly should also share some medical ailments, high blood pressure or aching joints, the club members loved to weigh in on that kind of thing. Maureen smiled at her own pun. But regardless of the ultimate outcome of Dolly's journey, Maureen and her Marvellous Tim Noakes ENDORSED Meal Plans would be right there by her side.

Maureen had a purpose for the first time in years. She wasn't just an aimless, bored, lonely housewife, an empty nester, or a widow anymore; now, for the first time in years, she was a woman of action, a businesswoman even.

THE HIJACKERS

'So, where are we going now?' Thabo asked, steering their new old car through the streets of Khayelitsha.

'I need a beer,' Papsak said. 'Let's go to Sista's shebeen.'

'And what are we going to do with *him* while we're in a shebeen?' Thabo pointed at Uncle Mlungu, who was propped up in the back seat, his sunglassed head tilted against the window.

'Can't he wait in the car?'

'You don't think someone will notice a mlungu sleeping in the back seat of a skorokoro outside a shebeen in Khayelitsha, Papsak?'

'It's not a skorokoro, it's a classic car.'

'Plus Lefty said this guy is famous. I checked, and Lefty is right, he's a dieting guru. People everywhere know who he is. Every single day people lose hundreds of kilograms on this diet he came up with. You should try it, Papsak!' joked Thabo, prodding his comrade in the gut.

Papsak swatted Thabo's hand away, 'How do you know all that stuff about him?'

'I googled him on the internet,' Thabo said.

'How?'

Thabo pulled the Samsung out of his pocket and held it up. His car seat was reclined as far back as it would go, and he was riding low, his elbow balanced on the open window, like he'd seen them do in R&B music videos.

'Where did you get that phone?' Papsak asked.

'It was in Uncle's pocket,' Thabo said. 'Remember, you were smoking, you didn't want to check his pockets, so I did it and this is what I found. Your loss! You see, smoking is bad for you!'

'Hey, if you found it on Uncle, then it's half mine,' Papsak complained.

'What do you want me to do, cut it in half?' Thabo shouted.

'No, but you must share it fifty-fifty with me.'

'How are we going to do that?' Thabo asked.

'I use it half the day, you use it the other half of the day,' Papsak said.

'We've got bigger problems right now than how to cut a phone in half. You heard Lefty, anyone can recognise Uncle Mlungu, and the cops will be looking everywhere for him. We need to get rid of him fast.'

'I don't know what to do! If you're so clever, why don't you google it on your new cell phone?' sulked Papsak, pointedly looking out the window.

The phone started to ring and both men leaned over to look at it.

'Who is it?' Papsak asked.

'How should I know? It's the same number that was ringing earlier,' Thabo shrugged.

'What are you going to do?'

'Just ignore it.'

After a few moments, the phone stopped ringing, and then came the bleep of a new message. Neither man took any notice. They drove for a few minutes in silence, then Thabo asked: 'Okay, so where are we going to dump Uncle?'

THE CO-AUTHORS

'I'm glad you could come,' said Shaun as he closed the door. 'How are you holding up?'

'I think I'm in shock, I still can't believe it,' Marco said. 'It was all over the radio on the way here.'

Marco walked through to Shaun's lounge, where Xolisa was sitting bolt upright in an armchair, a blanket wrapped around her. Marco bent and gave her a quick, awkward hug and a kiss on the top of her head.

Sounds of sobbing came from a laptop on the coffee table. 'Hi Shireen, how are you holding up, cara?' Marco asked, waving at the woman in the Skype window.

Shireen had chestnut hair billowing around her face. She held clumps of tissues in her fingers, the nails painted the brightest red possible. At the sight of Marco, she buried her head in the tissues and howled even louder.

'I just ca … ca … can't be … believe we'll ne … never see him again,' she hiccupped. 'It all feels … so … so final!'

'Breathe love, breathe,' Marco said.

He took in the deep bags under Xolisa's eyes. Her face seemed even tenser than usual. He squeezed her shoulder gently, unsure how else to comfort her. They weren't usually a touchy-feely group. Shireen continued sobbing in the background, pulling tissue after tissue out of a box, like a magician with a never-ending handkerchief.

'The press are already going batshit crazy, and this is only the beginning. My husband had to unplug our home phone. How's your phone?' Xolisa asked Marco.

'Non-stop, I had to turn my cell off, and we had to take our home line off the hook too, all the calls were driving Chris nuts. I don't even know where they got our number from, it's not like it's listed. They've even been calling the restaurant. Soon they'll be camping out outside our homes.'

'Can I get you guys a cup of coffee?' Shaun offered.

'How about something a little stronger?' Xolisa said.

'Jesus, Xolisa, it's the middle of the day,' Shaun objected.

'Actually, I could also do with a drink,' Marco said. 'Any more info?' He nodded towards the massive flat-screen TV mounted on the wall, the sound muted. The image on the screen was of a journalist speaking earnestly into a microphone as she stood on the pavement across the road from Noakes's house, which was under police guard and heavily cordoned off with tape.

There was a fresh barrage of wailing from Shireen. Shaun reached for the remote and unmuted the sound, and the journalist's voice spiked through the kind of surround sound only bachelors with no kids have.

'... Noakes's domestic worker pressed the panic button at ten to three this morning after she discovered the body in the kitchen. Gloria Ngeju was returning to her employer's home after a trip to the Eastern Cape for an aunt's funeral. In a bizarre twist, police have been unable to locate the whereabouts of the body, after the ambulance transporting the body to the mortuary was hijacked in Salt River. At this time it's uncertain whether the murder and the hijacking are related. In a media briefing with the police earlier today, Detective September, the lead detective in the case, made a brief statement to the press...'

The camera cut to footage of a policeman with a moustache and a boep, speaking into a microphone at a press briefing: 'Until we are able to recover the body and perform an autopsy, the cause of death remains unknown. We are doing everything we can to track down the hijackers and other persons of interest.' The detective added, 'We are also trying urgently to reach Mrs Noakes, who appears to have gone missing.'

The camera cut jerkily back to the journalist outside the Noakes's home. 'Police request that anyone with any information that might lead to the recovery of the body or capture of the hijackers please step forward to assist them in this matter. Likewise, if anyone has information on Mrs Noakes's whereabouts...'

'Nothing new,' Shaun said, muting the television, so that Shireen's sobs were audible once again. Now she was wailing about Noakes's wife. 'I ca ... can't stand it if so ... something's happened to her too, she's s ... s ... so amazing!'

'Shireen, enough already,' snapped Shaun, 'I can barely hear myself think.'

'Don't shout at Shireen,' Marco shot back. 'It's okay, cara, you cry as much as you need to.'

Shireen amped up her sobbing a few notches.

'She's doing my head in!' Shaun leaned over and turned down the sound on the computer. Then he took three glasses and a bottle of Johnnie Walker Black Label from the glass-fronted liquor cabinet. 'I've been checking the internet, but nobody is saying anything new, just the same story repeating over and over, peppered with interviews with friends, neighbours and people who knew him, and a whole bunch of crime experts offering random theories. My guess is there will be more of the same until some new information swoops in to take its place.'

Xolisa sighed loudly.

'This is nuts,' Marco said, 'I spoke to him just the other night.'

'When?' Shaun asked, whipping his head around to look at Marco.

'How did he seem?' Xolisa's voice was tense.

'I don't know, I'd just come home from the gym. We spoke on the phone. He seemed ... well, to be honest, he seemed normal. He was heading off to some event, I can't remember which one. I wish I'd paid more attention. He was the keynote speaker.'

'Of course he was,' sniped Xolisa, and Marco intercepted Shaun shooting a glare at her.

'I can't believe he's gone,' Marco said again.

'Well we'd all better get out of denial fast, because this *has* happened, and a lot of people are going to be asking us questions, so we should probably get our stories straight,' Shaun said.

'What do you mean, we should get our stories straight?' Marco asked. 'You keep saying that.'

He caught another loaded glance between Xolisa and Shaun as she took her drink from him, their hands brushing. He tried to make sense of it as Shaun handed him his own whisky.

'Usually when someone's murdered, that person's spouse or lover is always the first suspect, and we're as much in bed with the guy as anyone else,' Shaun said.

'Oh God, what if it was his wife?' bawled Shireen. Everyone ignored her.

'Shaun's right,' Xolisa said, 'we do need to get our stories straight, and prepare for the worst.'

'Each of us is going to have to be able to account for our whereabouts last night,' Shaun added. 'Well, probably not you, Shireen, since you're in Joburg.'

'It's the suddenness of the whole thing,' Shireen sobbed, pulling five more tissues out of the box and clasping them to her face.

'Hang on, we don't even know for sure that it's murder yet, do we?' Marco said. 'You heard the detective, they haven't confirmed cause of death. It seems like you're all jumping to massive conclusions here. What if he died of natural causes? It could have been a heart attack, or a stroke maybe, he's not that young anymore.'

'For God's sake, I saw pictures of a bloodied face on Twitter!' Shaun snarled.

'So what? That's not conclusive proof that he was murdered, or that it wasn't a home invasion gone wrong. Unless you know something you're not telling us?' Marco prodded.

'Wait, what are you getting at?' Shaun asked.

'Just that you seem very convinced that he was murdered, Shaun.

What do you know that we don't?'

'Let me get this straight. Now you're accusing me of murdering the Prof?' Shaun snorted.

'Like you said, it wouldn't hurt if we all had our stories straight. So where were *you* last night?' Marco asked.

'I could ask you the same thing,' Shaun said.

'I've got nothing to hide. After the restaurant closed, I was at home with Chris all night,' Marco snapped. 'But you haven't answered my question. Where were you? What are you not telling us, Shaun?'

'If you must know, Marco, we were together,' Shaun pointed at Xolisa, whose head was bowed.

'What do you mean, you were together?' said Marco, surprised. Even Shireen stopped howling and looked up from her tissues.

'It just so happens that we went to Tasha's at the Waterfront to get a bite to eat.'

'Alone?' Marco asked, glancing between the two of them. 'Wait, since when do you two go out for dinner together alone?'

'And after dinner we came back here, and neither of us left the house again until seven thirty this morning.' Shaun sounded almost proud.

'You two ... since when? Xoliswa, what about your husband? I ... I...' Marco gaped and pointed, moving his finger between them, unable to find the words he needed to finish the sentence. 'Hang on a minute. Ha! I see what's going on here...' he trailed off.

'What's that supposed to mean?' Shaun asked.

'This is all very convenient. On the very night something happens to the Prof, you two are suddenly an item, out of nowhere, providing each other with the perfect alibi.'

'I don't like what you're insinuating.' Shaun stepped towards Marco, shoving him in the shoulder hard enough to propel the chef backwards.

'Guys, guys, stop it,' Xolisa said, her voice shaking.

'And I don't like what *you're* insinuating,' Marco said, pushing back at Shaun.

After that it was hard to tell who pushed who, or who had who by the collar: it all devolved quite quickly. Xolisa tried to pull the two men off each other as Shireen shrieked, and in the confusion of arms and fists and shouts, someone's elbow smashed into Xolisa's chin, and she went barrelling backwards and smashed down onto the glass coffee table, sending the laptop flying. The two men let go of each other and raced over to her. Xolisa took Shaun's hand and let him help her to her feet amid the broken shards of glass.

'I think you'd better go,' Shaun spat at Marco.

'I'm so sorry! Are you okay, Xolisa? God, there's glass everywhere! You're not bleeding or hurt?' Marco asked.

'I'm fine,' Xolisa said. 'He's right, you should probably go,' she added quietly.

'What's going on? Guys? I can't see anything! What happened? Someone turn me round!' Shireen was still shrieking from the laptop, which had spun away from them and was facing a wall.

Marco dropped his head and made for the door. He caught a glimpse of himself in Shaun's hallway mirror. His shirt was torn and he was going to have a massive shiner in the morning, but those were the least of his problems.

'Hi, it's me calling again. I called a few times earlier and left a couple of messages about the thing. You're still not answering your phone, so I'm leaving another message.' Trevor suddenly remembered the cockney accent and slipped into it for the rest of the message. 'Maybe you're restin' up after a big night out ... um, I know you were busy umm ... doing your photography late last night, mate. I really 'ope you got all the "shots" you was after, innit. But call me as soon as you get this, guv'nor. I just want to check about the final payment, and make sure that everyfink went as planned, is in tip-top shape, wiv the you-know-what, orright? It woz you what did it, right?' Trevor realised he was rambling again. 'I 'ope you've still got the number for me pager. I keep it wiv me all the time, so gi' us a tinkle when you get this please. Just in case you've lost it, it's 539462. Any time is fine; I'm a night owl. Thanks, mate.'

Trevor put down the phone, and then worried about his accent. What if it was too good, and the hitman didn't recognise his voice? What if he had no clue who this weird cockney guy who kept calling was, and that's why he hadn't answered any of his calls or paged him? Trevor considered saying his name next time he called, but what if someone was listening in? He wished he'd chosen a different accent. His Spanish wasn't bad, and it somehow seemed to have more gravitas than cockney, in light of the subject matter. 'Uno cervesa, por favor,' he tried out loud for nobody in particular. But it was too late, there was no going back: he couldn't turn into a Spanish cockney guy at this stage. What was done was done, and he was going to have to live with the consequences, in more ways than one.

Where was that damn hitman? Had he done it, or had someone else pipped him to the post? According to the internet, there were quite a few candidates for the job.

Trevor checked his pager for the millionth time, but there was still no word. Who carried a pager anyway? It had seemed like a good idea at the time.

THE FANS

THE BANTING FOR LIFE FACEBOOK PAGE

Natasja Kleviansky
Hello Banting family. Bullet Proof Coffee is my new most favourite thing in the whole world. I <3 <3 <3 it. And I even heard that it's supposed to make your brain work better, BONUS! One cup and I'm full till lunch time and sharp as anything.
Like 169

Fran Kaplan Please share your recipe. I'm new to Banting and I've never even heard of bullet proof coffee before, but it sounds great.
Like 25

Natasja Kleviansky Sure thing Fran Kaplan
Bullet Proof Coffee, Natasja style:
One cup of coffee
1 tsp butter
1 tsp coconut oil
1 tsp xylitol
1 raw egg
half a tsp vanilla essence
a pinch of cinnamon or hazlenut or cocco (depending what I'm in the mood for)
a little bit of cream

So I make my coffee, like normal. Then I put the coffee and butter and oil and the egg in the blender. Mix it till there's a layer of foam on top like a cupuchino. **Then sprinkle some grated hazelnut** or cinnamon or cocco) and the sweetener and dollop of cream is the cherry on top ☺. **I like to sprinkle it on in the shape of a heart like they do in the Vida. Very professional. This is the perfect breakfast (sometimes if I'm late for work I can even take it in the MyCiti with me – see it travels too). This breakfast can last me till two o clock on some days, before I'm hungry again.**
Like 12

Fran Kaplan Ugh, that sounds a bit yuck.
Like 26

Natasja Kleviansky I know, but it's absolutely delicious. I promise. Try it you will love it.
Like 4

De Wet Barry How can you people swop recipes when the Prof is lying dead somewhere?
Like 28

Charte Nortje Ja it's a travesty. You should be ashamed of yourselves. It's not right.
Like 21

Natasja Kleviansky Oh please, I never even met him. Get a life. It's sad that he's gone, but it doesn't mean we all have to stop what we're doing. Life goes on. Haven't you ever watched The Lion King? It's the circle of life.
Like 10

Eldridge Pieterson How many cups of bulletproof coffee do you think I can have in a day? I currently have more than two cups. do you think it will affect my weight loss?
Like 2

Charissa Naidoo Don't you get the shakes with so much coffee Eldridge Pieterson? And I don't mean diet shakes har har har. For me it depends if I'm having it as a meal or over and above a meal. I find that if I have it over and above a meal, my weight loss is not as good. And I also think you negative moaners should get a life, we need to keep up with the Profs lifestyle in tribute to him.
Like 7

Maureen Ewehout Hello Natasja Kleviansky, Eldridge Pieterson, Fran Kaplan and Charissa Naidoo. As a purveyor of Tim Noakes ENDORSED Marvellous meal plans, I would suggest that you only go with one cup of BPC in the day. Perhaps you could include coffee in your dessert option, if you're really missing the caffeine. I have a Banting coffee cheesecake recipe that is to die for, that I sell as part of my individually tailored Noakes ENDORSED Marvellous meal plans. (Direct message me if you'd like to find out more).
Like 17

Fran Kaplan you can eat cheesecake????? Cheesecake + coffee, two of my favourite things. I LOVE THIS LIFESTILE!
Like 29

Natasja Kleviansky Thank you so much **Maureen Ewehout** I will definately get in touch with you.

Like 1

Dot Swart is their a recipe for bullet proof tea? Or is tea a carb?

Like 0

View 210 more comments

THE CO-AUTHORS

Wednesday 3:47pm

Xolisa rolled onto her back and pulled the duvet up to cover herself, then silently clenched her buttocks for three reps of twenty. Her chin still hurt, and her leg was bruised and aching, but as a long-distance marathon runner, Iron Woman competitor and personal trainer to a number of celebrity clients, she knew better than anybody how important it was to push through the pain and keep her body moving.

'Was that as good for you as it was for me?' Shaun asked, sliding an arm across her waist.

Xolisa ignored him and did three reps of fifteen side-leg lifts. Any opportunity to work her quads.

'Babe, did you try reiki yet, like I suggested?' Shaun asked, as he massaged her shoulders. 'I know we've talked about this before, but your second chakra is completely blocked. I really wish you'd come and see me at my practice. Why don't you call Desray in the morning and set up an appointment? We can do some life coaching for you as well.'

Xolisa gritted her teeth, brushed his hands off her shoulders and did three reps of fifteen butterfly crunches.

'We can spend some time figuring out your career goals. I've got a great new set of motivational cards. We can also look at your hopes, your driving forces, and where you see yourself in five years' time. Nothing is impossible with a dream and a plan.'

'I'll tell you where I see myself in five years' time,' Xolisa growled. 'Not a blurry smudge at the back of a group author photograph, that's where. And not the token black woman in a team of egotistical neocolonising writers, that's for sure.'

'No babe, c'mon, you have to put positive thoughts out there. You're one of the co-authors of the top-selling lifestyle book of our generation. And you're not a token; you're tougher than the lot of us, you've got a successful personal training business, and don't forget your buns of steel,' said Shaun, squeezing her bottom. 'I mean, you don't have as much as an inch of cellulite anywhere on your body.'

Xolisa pulled one knee up to her chest in a stretch. 'Please, I barely had anything to do with that book in the end, and you know it. Where's my chapter on lunges? Hey? And what about the chapter I wrote on the value of cardio, or the effect of weight-bearing exercise on osteoporosis and weight loss? Nowhere! Lying on the cutting-room floor, right next to the chunk they photoshopped off Marco's body, that's fucking where.'

'You see, it's this kind of negativity we can work on together when you come to my practice to clear your chakras. I can offer you some real guidance and life coaching.'

'Oh for fuck's sake, Shaun. Catch a fucking wake-up,' Xolisa snapped, getting up and taking the duvet with her into the bathroom, leaving Shaun naked and shrivelled on the bed.

THE EX-PUBLISHER

'You know what happened to me yeshterday?' Frank slurred, spilling his drink as he waved his glass at the man sitting two barstools down from him. 'You'll like thish one, it's really fucking hilarioush,' he said.

The man turned towards Frank and nodded him on cautiously, not willing to shift a seat closer in case there was another snub coming.

'Sho I take shandwiches to work theshe days, you know? I haven't alwaysh, I ushed to eat out for lunch every day and twice on Shundays. But theshe days I'm on a budget. So it'sh peanut butter and jam, shometimes cheese. But anyway, I had a shandwich left over, pb and jam, and I'm on my way home from work, sho I give it to this homelessh guy on the pavement jusht sitting there, being poor ash fuck.

'There I am thinking I'm being the humani-fucking-tarian of the year, but you know what he did? Go on, take a guesh, guesh what the fucker shaid?' Frank noticed he was spilling his drink as he gesticulated, and licked at his arm, not wanting to miss a drop. Then he took another large gulp, drained his glass and yelled for the barman to pour him another.

The man shrugged.

'Thish fucking begging guy took one look at the shandwich, and shaid, no thanksh, I'm trying to cut down on my carbsh.'

The man sitting two barstools down snorted, and even the barman smirked.

'Yeah, laugh,' Frank said, 'but you shee, it'sh not actually funny. Where'sh my fucking drink?' he bellowed at the barman again, who raised an eyebrow at him as he refilled his glass.

'That fucker ruined my life,' Frank moaned.

'The homeless man?' asked the man two barstools down.

'No, you fucking moron, that dead Banting professhor, the sho-called guru that everyone ish praying to theshe daysh,' said Frank, putting air quotation marks around the word 'guru' and spilling more of his drink in the process.

'Oh you mean Tim Noakes? The guy who wrote that diet book?'

'That'sh the one!' Frank said. 'Can I tell you a shecret?' He glanced over each shoulder. 'I could have published hish book. But it wash the one that got away. It'sh the shaddest story you'll ever hear. I passhed on it.'

'You passed on it?' the man asked.

'Yup! Guessh what'sh got two thumbs and passhed on the gooshe that laysh the golden fucking eggsh? Thish guy!' Frank pointed his two thumbs at himself, almost swaying off his barstool in the process.

'I'm a publisher,' Frank slurred. 'I mean I wash a publisher, before I let the big one get away. The professhor wanted me to publish it and I turned him down. I told him it was a fad. I shaid nobody would ever buy into eating pure fat. I shaid it was the dumbest idea I'd ever heard. I shaid doctors around the world would laugh him out of the room, and then shue him for malpractice. Ha ha ha, who's the arshehole now? Two hundred thoushand copiesh shold, and counting, plus all the shpin-offs, and thish ish only the beginning, they predict it'll shell millions. Thish ish the next big thing. And what did I do? I turned it down. Then I losht my job, and my wife left me and took the houshe and my car. She even kept the dog, and my kidsh won't talk to me, they shay I'm a drunk, ha! All because of that shtupid professhor and his shtupid fucking diet book.'

'I'm sorry,' said the man. 'But we all make mistakes, I should know...'

Frank interrupted him, 'This wash more than a fucking mishtake, buddy, it's a tragedy, a cataclyshm, an apocalypshe. Genoshide.' Frank's tongue felt too fat for his mouth, and he was struggling to find the right words to explain himself. He prodded at his tongue with his finger to see if it was actually as large as it felt.

'Well, it's hardly genoci...'

'Ish a fuck-up, that'sh what it ish,' Frank interrupted him. 'And who ended up publishing him? Some mom-and-pop team. It'll be Lamborghinish and caviar for them forever, while I eat shandwiches not even a homelesh pershon wantsh. I'm glad I punched him, and I'm glad he'sh dead.'

Frank's reluctant confidant stared him, and took another slow sip of his beer. 'You can't mean that...?' he started.

'I'm the arshehole who joined the ranksh of the record label that turned down The Beatlesh, or the company who told the guy who invented the pershonal computer that they'd never shell more than ten.'

'But how could you have known this diet book was going to be such a big hit?' asked the man two barstools down.

'I should have known!' Frank sighed. 'It was my businessh to know. And now the bashtard is finally dead, the day I've been plotting and planning and dreaming of. I thought ... I hoped now that he'sh gone I'd shtop being reminded of him everywhere. But it turnsh out the joke ish on me. I'd never conshidered how it would play out, but hish death ish going to make him even more popular, bigger shales, more fansh, more publishity, greater fame. I forgot the number one rule in publishing – after don't let the big sheller get away – there'sh no shuch thing as bad publishity!' Frank snorted. 'Ha, shitty! Exactly, publishitty!'

The man looked at Frank pityingly.

'Another drink, for fuck'sh shake, barman!' Frank shouted, downing the dregs he'd managed not to spill. 'And one for my friend here.'

'Don't you think you've had enough?' the barman asked. 'And maybe you should get that hand looked at, it doesn't look so good.'

'I'll be fine,' Frank slurred, wincing as he shoved his injured hand into his pocket. 'Now do your fucking job and get me another drink.'

THE WIDOW

The Banting For Life page was exploding with news, views, suspicious comments, crazy conspiracy theories and opinions on Professor Noakes's murder. There were thousands of new comments. Maureen scrolled through them, her heart pounding in her throat.

Fourie De Villiers
Whoever did it deserves to get the electric chair.
Like 102

Nonwabisa Cele I don't think we have the electric chair in South Africa.
Like 23

Fourie De Villiers Well then, they should extradite that person to a country that does.
Like 97

Tania Southby I still just can't believe the news, my heart is broken in two, this country is going to the dogs I tell you. Canada, here I come.
Like 17

Giselle Gaffrey What did I miss? What happened?
Like 0

Refilwe Jwara Didn't you hear **Giselle Gaffrey** have you been under a rock or something? Tim Noakes was murdered this morning in his own home. They say it was someone with an axe.
Like 27

Celeste Olson-McCallister I heard it was the co-authors, they murdered him so they could get his royalties. I heard it was with a panga.
Like 67

Giselle Gaffrey Nooooooooooooo! This can't be happening.
Like 19

Chetna Pillay That's not how it works at all, how stupid can you get? Now that he's dead he still gets his royalties, they just go to his family or next of kin.
Like 47

Godfrey Mandikele Then maybe his family or next of kin did it?
Like 29

Theo Williams They should make a statue of him or something.
Like 68

Barend du Plessis I think it was the government who did it. He was becoming too powerful. They don't like that.
Like 90

Maureen Ewehout Well, I'm of course devastated that he's gone, I've been crying all day, he was my friend and mentor. But if you really think about it, he wasn't a young man, he spent his life in service to runners and sports people, and now to all of us. He had a good innings (he was a great advocate of cricket too) and look at the legacy he's left behind. Some people can spend their entire lives on this planet and never do a quarter as much good as he has. All I'm saying is he had a good run, he was in his sixties after all, not a young man. It's a huge tragedy of course, but imagine if he had been in his twenties ... we were lucky to have him as long as we did. And his legacy lives on in this phenomenal new eating lifestyle.
Like 41

Maureen considered adding in a small punt for her ENDORSED meal plans, but she decided she'd already made quite a noise about them today, so once she'd posted her comment she logged out, then logged back in as Lydia Steenberg, and got Lydia to 'like' Maureen's post. Then she logged in as Sizwe, then Dolly, and even Herman, giving herself as many 'likes' as possible.

As she'd predicted, business was flying. In the wake of the Prof's death, interest in Banting had soared to new heights. Maureen had already sold twenty ENDORSED meal plans that day. She hadn't earned her own money since she'd been in her twenties, working at the hotel in Somerset West, where she did their books and worked behind the bar because her dad knew the owner. That was where she'd met Gus, and the rest was history.

Maureen replied carefully to each of the meal plan direct messages with her standard copy-and-pasted response, outlining information on her background, her 'partnership' with the Professor, as well as what the meal plans entailed, and then of course, the most important part; her banking details so they could make prompt payment if they wanted to move forward, enrich their lives and reach their goals.

As she typed, she caught a movement out of the corner of her eye and let out a sharp screech. She dived for her knobkierie, and WHAM! If there was one thing she couldn't stand, it was cockroaches. Then she took the weapon into the kitchen and rinsed it off under the tap. She made herself a cup of tea, then went back to work.

Maureen logged out of her own Facebook account, then logged back in as Lydia Steenberg once again. She no longer even had to check for Lydia's password on the pinboard, she knew it off by heart, as she should, considering that over the last few days she'd logged in as lydiasteenberg1987@gmail.com more often than she'd logged in as herself. Although only a few hours had passed since their first conversation, Maureen was anxious to see if Benjamin had written to her again.

She tapped in Lydia's password, 'pretty young blonde', then clicked straight through to her messages and reread the conversation between Benjamin and Lydia for the fifth time. Was he flirting with her? Of course he was. She wasn't so old and naïve that she couldn't see that. She flushed and reminded herself it was Lydia he was flirting with: young, firm, imaginary Lydia, not old, baggy, fraudulent Meal Plan Maureen.

When Benjamin had first struck up the conversation with Lydia, Maureen had decided not to respond. But he seemed pleasant enough, none of that 'Hello Dear I wanna be yr special friend, write to me and I will send my picture' stuff, so she had snooped around on his page a bit, checking out the few pictures he'd posted. He'd looked so young and virile and handsome, she couldn't not respond, could she? That would be rude, considering the time he'd taken to write to her. Anyway, what harm would it do? It was a great opportunity for her to encourage him along the way, even share some tips.

In fact, she told herself, as the more experienced and successful Banter, she wasn't lying so much by pretending to be Lydia, as helping. It was obviously the right thing, the humane thing to do. She would also be able to punt her ENDORSED meal plans, which had been the main aim of inventing Lydia in the first place. Reassured, she had typed up her first slightly flirty response to Benjamin on Lydia's behalf.

Wait a minute. There was a small fly in the ointment. What if he asked to meet Lydia, or even worse, asked her out on a date? Surely that's where this whole thing was heading, for him at least? He was half her age, maybe even younger. She was certain he would not take kindly to discovering that he'd inadvertently been flirting with a woman who was old enough to be his mother – possibly even his grandmother. What did the kids on the internet say these days? She was 'catfishing' him. He might even call the police. But it was too late to back out now, she thought, as she logged out of Lydia's account, and then back in as Sizwe.

THE CO-AUTHORS

'Oh my goodness, Marco, what happened to your face?'

Marco winced as his husband touched his cheek.

'It's nothing. Shaun and I got into it, he hit me.' Marco dropped his keys on the table by the front door and eased off his jacket.

'That walking steroid, how dare he lay a hand on you!' yelled Chris. 'We'll sue the pants off his tiny wrinkly balls!'

'Oh sweetheart,' Marco laughed, then winced again.

'I'll get you an ice pack,' said Chris, heading for the kitchen, Marco following him.

'I got in a few good shots too, babe, you would have been proud of me. He's going to be just as sore. But Xolisa tried to stop us, and she got pushed by accident. I feel terrible about it. She fell onto that horrible eighties glass coffee table of Shaun's and broke it. There were shards of glass everywhere.'

'Oh shit, is she okay?' Chris asked.

'I think so.'

'Don't worry, she's tough as Zuma, that one. But what on earth were you two fighting about?'

Marco sucked in air as Chris placed an icy bag of frozen peas against his bruised cheek. 'He's just such a monumental dick!'

'Tell me something I don't know,' said Chris. He paused before asking, 'Do you think they suspect anything?'

'What? About the Prof and me? No, I don't think so. Well, nothing they could make stick.'

'You're definitely sure they don't know about the new book you were doing with him?' Chris asked.

'There's no way they could know. I seriously doubt the Prof would have told them. And he and I were the only ones who knew about it at this stage.'

'What about the publishers?' Chris asked.

'Absolutely not. The Prof and I had agreed to wait till it was finished and good to go before we pitched it. No leaks until it was one hundred per cent ready. There are just so many copycats out there right now.'

'And what about the arguments you were having with the Prof?' Chris asked. 'Do any of them know about those?'

'Nobody could have known, unless he told his wife.'

'Any sign of her yet?'

'Not that I know of. I hope she's okay.'

'So now what?' Chris asked, pouring a glass of wine and handing it to Marco, then pouring himself one.

'We go on as planned, nothing changes. Why would it?' Marco snapped.

'Are you going to get the new book published under your name?'

'Yup,' said Marco. 'We get the book published under my name. It will all be very sad and unfortunate, but the timing is perfect. I'll say that the Prof would have wanted me to go ahead and share his – our – my vision with the world. I'll dedicate it to him, make it a tribute. The media will lap it up, and I think the punters will go ape-shit for it.'

'Not to mention the fans,' Chris said.

'Not to mention the fans,' Marco agreed.

'And we won't have to share the royalties with anyone this time.'

'That's what I like to hear. Cheers! Here's to you.' Chris clinked his glass against Marco's.

'Cheers,' said Marco, gingerly taking a sip. 'Oh, wait, you won't believe this.'

'What?'

'They're fucking each other.'

'Who?'

'Shaun and Xolisa.'

'No way!

'Way!'

'How long has that been going on?'

'I don't know, they say they were together last night and that she slept over at his place,' Marco explained.

'Wow. I mean, I knew Xolisa and Cyril were having problems, but I didn't realise ... I didn't see that coming.'

'Me neither,' Marco said.

'She's so bony and full of angles, I can't picture her having sex with anyone.'

'I know, right?'

'What did Shireen say?' Chris asked.

'She was on Skype, I'm not even sure she heard. She cried through the whole conversation.'

'Typical.'

Marco nodded.

'The press is already having a field day with the murder. If you were to tell them about Shaun and Xolisa's affair, that would really make their heads explode. Honey, maybe you can get an exclusive in *You* magazine with the story. They'd definitely pay for it.'

'Do you think so?'

'Absolutely, but we'd better move on it, and call your agent straight away, in case Shireen has the same idea.'

'You're a genius.'

'How's your face feeling?' Chris asked.

'Better now,' smiled Marco, holding out his glass for a refill. 'And hopefully better than that wanker's.'

THE FANS

THE BANTING FOR LIFE FACEBOOK PAGE

Sizwe Madonda
Molweni everybody in Banting land. I wanted to update all you kind supportive people on my journey. Things have been going very well for me. Despite being a man who always loved his pap, eish how I miss it. But I have managed to lose thirty-two kilograms in total.

This Banting is really for me. If my ex-wife had to see me now! I used to get such bad indigestion I would be crying, Aikona! But now this is much better. Also my aches and pains are less than before. This week I can proudly say that I have lost another two kilograms. But I have a secret Banting weapon. I couldn't have done any of this without Maureen Ewehout's Marvellous Noakes ENDORSED Meal Plans. They are amazing. I learnt about cauli-rice and cauli-mash when I first started out, but now she has introduced me to cauli-pap! It's so nca!

One day someone must just invent cauli-umqombothi and then I'll bring out my vuvuzela! Go Chiefs!
Like 209

Tina Nortje You are inspiring1
Like 17

Neil Kleynhans So impressed and pleased for you. I love the idea of cauli-pap. Well done.
Like 14

Maureen Ewehout I'm so pleased it's working for you Sizwe Madonda, I'm proud of you. I'll get to work on creating a Marvellous ENDORSED Meal Plan with cauli-umqombothi immediately. ☺
Like 27

Thandi Malibongwe That sounds nca, share the recipe.
Like 13

Zwelethu Magona Cauli-pap? Are you sure you're black? Abelungu bayaphambana.
Like 7

THE EX-PUBLISHER

'That's it, you've had enough! I'm cutting you off,' the barman said, swiping his cloth along the counter. Frank had managed to get more of his most recent drink on the bar than into his mouth.

'You're damn right, I've had enough!' Frank shouted, slamming his left fist on the bar counter. He was slurring even worse, and he kept sliding off his barstool. There was clearly something wrong with it.

Frank turned to speak to his new friend, the man sitting two barstools down from him. 'I'll tell you what I've had enough of, that fucking Tim Noakesh, that'sh who. Hashn't he had enough? Enough fame, enough money, enough ruining other people'sh lives...'

Dimly Frank realised the man two stools down from him wasn't there anymore. So he heaved himself up and onto the foot rungs of his barstool, and shouted out to everyone in the bar: 'I losht everything thanksh to that fraud Noakesh and his hair-brained money-making shcheme. I had to go work at a fucking chain bookshtore, for fuck'sh shake! Two yearsh ago I was one of thish country'sh greatesht publishers. I had a corner office and my own PA. And then I turned down one manushcript. One! I thought it was just another diet fad, and a crazy one, too. How wash I to know it would make millionsh? Sho I punched him in the face, I punched him and I punched him and I punched him, I punched that professhor until he fell over. Then I shtood on him, and I kicked him and kicked him.'

By now Frank was staggering around trying to demonstrate his ninja kicking technique, but he couldn't get his legs to co-operate.

'Wait, are you saying you attacked Tim Noakes?' asked the barman.

'Yesh! In the fashe!' Frank roared. 'Ha, he killed my career and now he'sh dead! Good riddansh!'

'My wife lost thirty-three kilos on that diet,' the barman said. 'That man is a national hero. They should have put him in parliament. He would have shut down the gravy train one time. You sit down over there and don't move a muscle, I'm calling the cops.'

'Call them!' Frank shouted, 'I'm glad I did it. I'd do it again!' Then he tried to sit on his barstool, missed, and collapsed in a cursing heap on the floor.

THE HIJACKERS

'So is this the Rondebosch Common?' Papsak asked.

'Ewe,' Thabo said.

'Okay, so then why are you driving around and around, you're mos wasting petrol and making my head spin. Let's dump him already.'

'Don't be an idiot your whole life, Papsak. I'm looking for a more private place. Look at these people coming past all the time. See, they're all running around and around, they keep coming back, the same ones. I need to find somewhere we can stop and get Uncle Mlungu out of the car so that none of these people will see us.'

'What if we carry him between us and pretend we're going for a walk, like we did earlier to take the taxi to Lefty's place? Then we can just drop him when nobody is looking and run back to the car quickly?' Papsak suggested.

'You see all these people coming past us all the time?' Thabo asked.

'Ja-aaa?'

'They're runners, Papsak.'

'So what?'

'I read on the internet on my new Samsung that Uncle Mlungu is a professor of running, so I'm worried that if we take him out of gusheshe here, these people will all recognise him for sure. What if someone comes to ask him for his autograph? Then what, ne?'

'No man, we'd better get the hell out of here,' said Papsak. 'Is he a professor of surfing too?'

'No, I didn't see that on the phone.'

'Good, then maybe we can dump him in the sea and nobody will recognise him there.'

The phone in Thabo's pocket bleeped.

Papsak jumped. The runners were making him nervous. 'Who is it?'

Thabo took out the phone and smiled. 'It's a "please call me" from Cynthia. I left her a message.' He leaned back in his seat and dialled her number.

Papsak rolled his eyes and turned on the radio. Thabo slapped Papsak's hand away from the dial and clicked his tongue at him.

'Hi baby,' Thabo growled into the phone, making his voice sound as deep and sexy as possible.

...

'No, it's me, Thabo.' His voice rose back to normal pitch.

...

'Yes, me, Thabo, from the shebeen the other night, remember? I'm calling you from my new phone. I got it this morning, it's a Samsung. It's got unlimited airtime.'

...

'Yes, brand-new. It was on special.'

...

'It's almost as cool as my new gusheshe!'

...

'Yes, a car too.'

...

'So baby, I thought maybe we can go out together some time?'

...

'Yes, I can pick you up later, I'm just working now.'

...

'Yes, I've got a job.'

...

'No, it's a real job, Cynthia. Serious business. That's where I got the money for the car and the phone.'

...

'Umm ... my job? I've got my own business, baby, I'm a BEE.'

...

Papsak pointed theatrically at the clock on the dashboard.

'My friend Papsak says hi, my baby,' Thabo said, ignoring his buddy.

...

'Yes, he's here with me, we're working together.'

...

'No, we're not at the shebeen, I told you, we're at work. Why don't you believe me?'

...

'We're making money, I told you.'

...

'Where do you think the money for all this airtime comes from?'

...

'Okay, I'd better go back to work. I'll call you later.'

...

'Okay, I love you.'

...

'Don't you love me?'

...

'Fine then, I'll call you later, you can tell me you love me then. Bye.' Thabo hung up at last.

THE EX-PUBLISHER

'Can you open the window, pleashe,' Frank slurred, 'I think I'm going to be ... BLEURGGHHHH...'

'Great, just great!' sighed the cop in the passenger seat.

'Is he dead or did he just pass out back there? You'd better check. They're going to want this guy in one piece back at the station for questioning on the Noakes murder,' said the other cop, tapping down on the indicator.

The first cop craned his neck to check through the window into the back of the police van. 'I can see him breathing. But I think he may have pissed himself.'

'Sis man! It's your turn to hose out the van when we get back to the station.'

'I thought it was your turn.'

'I did it last time, when we picked up those bergies who'd been riding the blue train on Long Street.'

'Oh, that's right.'

'Do you think this oke murdered Noakes?'

'The barman did say he confessed a bunch of times, loud enough for the entire bar to hear; there were at least ten witnesses. One of them even filmed it on his cell phone.'

'Yeah, but the barman also said he'd been in there drinking hard the whole day,' said the driver, scratching his head.

'And did you see the state of his hand? He definitely punched something very recently. Plus he only told us he did it about sixteen times.'

'Yeah. And then he pissed himself and passed out. Super-reliable.'

'You have a point. Did you ever try that Banting thing yourself?' the passenger-seat cop asked. 'I've heard it's a miracle diet. You can eat bacon and fat and everything.'

'My mother-in-law does it. She says it's not a diet, it's a lifestyle.'

'And? Has she lost any weight on it?'

'Ja, a whole bunch, but she's still a cow.'

'Still … bacon. A diet that lets you eat bacon. That's a thing.'

THE FANS

THE BANTING FOR LIFE FACEBOOK PAGE

Lydia Steenberg
This has been a dreadful few days...there's been Professor Noakes's tragic murder, which I worry we may never get over. As well as the horrific disappearance of his body (only in South Africa!). And for the last straw my amazing cat, Ginger Mary, passed away earlier today. She was run over outside my flat. I know this isn't strictly Banting related, but the reason I'm telling you all this is, I have discovered that I am an emotional eater and if I had not adopted the Banting way, I probably would have consumed everything in sight today. But it has been quite the opposite. I know it will be difficult in terms of eating, and I'm sure I will have one or two high carb items to eat as I mourn, maybe even a little bit of ice cream later on tonight, but not so that it is out of control. I've been in distress before and the cravings were massive, but now I feel like I can manage it. I was looking at some photographs of Ginger Mary and me when she was just a kitten, and I can't believe how much weight I've lost in such a short space of time. I went from being a fat cat-owner to a thin cat-owner. Ginger Mary I will miss you lots, I know how much you liked the cream we are allowed to eat with the Banting Way, and I will think of you whenever I eat it. Thank you Banting friends for letting me vent. It's been a very very hard day.
Like 476
View 719 more comments

THE CEO

"Ello, it's me again,' Trevor whispered into the handset in his cockney accent, which he was definitely getting more adept at. 'This is the third message I'm leaving for you. You 'aven't made contact to collect the rest of your, er, renumeration. The job's been done, I saw it on the news, so I don't understand why you 'aven't been in touch. So gi' us a call, mate, and put me in the picture, orright? On the radio, they're saying the coppers 'ave arrested a suspect, and that 'e's confessed to killing the Professor. No uvver details, but let me know you're okay, there's a pal? I bloody well 'ope it's not you they've got banged up. It's just that it would explain why you 'aven't been in touch, so I'm a bit nervy. Is this a set-up? Because if it is, you'll never get away with it. If any of this leads back to me, I'm just saying ... if you rolled over on me to cut a deal for yourself ... I ... I wouldn't last in prison, I'm too white, my 'ands are too soft. So what I'm saying is, please, the second you get this, call me. Let me know what's goin' down and that it's not you in custody so I can stop worryin'. Orright, mate?'

Trevor put down the phone, then wiped his sticky hands down the sides of his dark-blue suit pants. Next time he'd bring some of that disinfectant they sold at the tills at Woolworths, the ones that didn't need water, where you just squeezed some onto your hands, rubbed them together and they were disinfected, the dirt gone.

For a split second Trevor fantasised about being the CEO of the company that made that clear disinfectant stuff, instead of being the head cheese at SnackCorp. That handwash company would be so easy to run. There wasn't a professor on earth who would make it his life's work to outlaw disinfectant. What a dream that job would be.

Trevor's cell phone rang in his breast pocket and he fumbled for it. It was his boss, Gunther. Again. He slipped the phone back into his pocket, letting the call go to message. Then he lifted the collar of his coat, shoved his hands deep into his pockets and headed back to his office. That would make it five times Gunther had tried to ring him today, and he'd left three messages. Trevor had only listened to one of them. Gunther wanted to let him know that they'd had an emergency board meeting and Trevor was urgently needed. This really did not bode well.

SnackCorp's stocks had plummeted by another ten points since the reports of Professor Noakes's death had gone viral. It wasn't what Trevor had expected, but maybe he just needed to hang in there. He was sure his thinking was still sound: out of sight, out of mind. As soon as the hype surrounding the Prof's death died down, things would go back to normal, and, according to Trevor's plan, the stupid diet would fade into obscurity, bread and cake sales would increase again – people were emotional eaters after all – and by the end of next year, they'd all be smoking cigars and golfing it up in Barbados again. Trevor just had to hang in there.

But he was very, very worried about the remaining loose ends. Why hadn't he thought through the whole thing more carefully?

Trevor's tummy rumbled: all this stress was making him hungry. He darted into the Debonairs outlet a few blocks from his office and ordered a Something Meaty Pizza, upgrading it from a standard to a large at the last minute.

THE CO-AUTHORS

'Are you sure you're okay?' Shaun asked, wrapping his arms around Xolisa.

'I'm fine. Please stop asking me.' Xolisa pulled away from him and went to sit in a chair across the room.

Shaun knelt beside her. 'Sweetheart, stop being so stubborn. Here, let me take a look at your chin. How's it feeling?'

Xolisa pushed his hand away. 'Shaun, I've changed my mind.'

Shaun sat back on his heels. 'About me looking at your chin?'

'No, about us,' Xolisa said, her voice flat. 'I think we should take a break from each other, at least until everything calms down.'

'But, but I thought...' Shaun stuttered in shock.

'I know, I thought too, but still, I've changed my mind.'

'But last night you said...'

'I know what I said, Shaun,' Xolisa interrupted, her tone sharper now.

'We were going to be an *IT* couple, you said! You said we were going to be the new face of Banting, together we were going to...'

'I know what I said, okay! But I've been thinking. We can't both be the face of Banting. Only one person can front this thing, that was the way it worked with the Prof, and it's why it worked so well.'

'And let me guess: you're that one person?' Shaun said, his voice suddenly laced with sarcasm.

'I suppose that remains to be seen, but I could be, if that's what the public wants,' she said. 'I'm not going to be the one giving you credibility, a nice little multi-racial package. Decolonisation, transformation, it's happening. Deal.'

'Why are you doing this, Xolisa?' Shaun pleaded. 'I don't understand where any of this is coming from. We're so good together!'

'Shaun, I have a public image to think of. Plus I need to try and make things work with my husband before throwing away three and a half years of marriage.'

'What? But you don't even like Cyril,' Shaun whined. 'How did you decide this overnight?'

'He's my husband, Shaun. Try to understand.'

'Well, I don't understand!' Shaun's voice started to climb. 'You can't even say his name out loud! You refer to him as your "husband".'

'That's because he is my husband,' Xolisa said, her voice now calm and even.

'But … we just told Marco and Shireen about us, what will we tell them now?'

'I don't care. You can tell them whatever you want. Tell them our chakras weren't aligning.'

'I can't believe you're doing this to me, Xolisa. Was this your plan all along? String me along, get me to do all the dirty work, then bail on me once the Prof was out the picture?'

Xolisa stood. 'No, Shaun, it's just the way things worked out. Of course I never meant to hurt you, and I care for you a great deal. I'm grateful for the things you chose to do for me. But with Noakes gone, everything's changed. I need to think very seriously about how I want to go forward with my career and my future.'

The couple stood staring at each other for a long minute, Shaun silent for once.

'I'm going to head home now,' Xolisa said, standing and picking up her overnight bag. Then she walked towards the door, limping slightly.

'No, wait…' he called, his voice desperate.

She reached the front door and opened it. 'One last thing, Shaun. That stubble you think is so sexy? It makes you look like a homeless person.'

'You're going to regret this,' Shaun threatened. 'You'll never get away with it.'

'That's the thing.' Xolisa looked back at him before she walked out the door. 'I think I will.'

THE CEO

Trevor sat on the hard, cold, plastic seat inside Debonairs, in the furthest corner at the very back of the restaurant, savouring his pizza. He hadn't had one in over six months (one failed attempt at a homemade pizza in the microwave at home, using cauliflower as the base, didn't count – cauli-pizza? Pizzauli? Caulizza? Picaulli?). He knew all too well that this comforting treat was going to wreak havoc on his digestion. There really was no such thing as a free meal.

Trevor wallowed in panic for the duration of a whole slice, and in self-pity for another slice. Then he turned the problem of the hitman over in his head. He'd handed over the first forty grand up front in cash and in person. The arrangement was that as soon as the job had been completed, the assassin would contact Trevor on his specially bought pager (he'd had to hunt it down on Ebay, they barely made them anymore) so that they could arrange a meeting to hand over the second forty grand. Noakes was definitely dead, so why hadn't the hitman called for his final payment yet? Did this mean he was the one in police custody? In which case, Trevor had much bigger problems.

Trevor pondered as he chomped through another piece of pizza his favourite way: folding it in half, then shoving it into his face, bite by delicious, cheesy, wheaty, constipating bite.

THE FANS

Wednesday 8:06pm

THE BANTING FOR LIFE FACEBOOK PAGE

Louise Wright
Oh my goodness, I just got on my scale. If you're thinking of doing it, do yourself a favour and don't. ☹
Like 2

Ashleigh Wyliman Oh yes, I so agree !!!! the scale is not always yur friend. mine lies to me constantley...... ☺

Anele Smit So true. maybe rather judge your wait from how your clothes feel and stay away from the scale. This coming from a new banter, only twelve days in so far, and loving it
Like 19

Sanette Der Walt I got on the scale yesterday, and I felt so awful and hopeless afterwards that I ate 100 grams of cheddar, 50 grams of salami and 60 grams of nuts!!! And all that right after I'd had a whole big Banting breakfast of scrambled eggies and smoked samon. ☹ I am feeling very despondent, but I don't want to give up. I just don't think I'll get on the scale again for a while!!!
Like 26

Dilly Heron thanks for the advice, I think Im going to wait for a while, maybe something like six months. maybe I wont even buy a scale till then to stop myself from being tempted to step on it and see. I dont want to fail at this.
Like 15

Ethel Markowitz good thinking **Dilly Heron** I'm going to do that too!
Like 1

Louise Wright I'm really hoping what I've got is just water retention or constipation, cos if I've put on weight for real I'm going to be really upset, I've stuck to the green list and everything.
Like 33

110

Daniel Gouws It could also be muscle gain. You know that muscle weighs much more than fat. Don't let it make you despondent.
Like 11

Louise Wright I know **Daniel Gouws** but it's an emotional roller coaster, up one day, down the next. Shooweee but it's not easy.
Like 10

Grant Spoegel I lost two pant sizes but ZERO kg, I would have been really upset about it, except my boyfriend kept telling me how fantastic I was looking and that really helped. Also TWO PANT SIZES!!!!. ☺
Like 29

Donna Ferguson I agree with Louise - I been trying out this lifestyle now for just over two months and have only lost 2kgs. But none of my clothes still fit me, I've had to go and get all new ones. I mostly got them from a second hand shop and from Pep, I didn't want to spend too much money on clothes, because I know I'm going to be losing a lot more weight on Bunting, and I can't wait until I'm finally down to my goal weight before I buy a whole new wardrobe – I would have to go to work naked otherwise. ☺ I haven't been thin in fifteen years, I can't wait. But don't get on the scale, it's disenheartening.
Like 24

Phillip White After reading this conversation, my scale is being repurposed,and I have found a better use for it, in the dustbin. haahahaha
Like 27

Samara Pillay Dilly Heron why 6 months? Is that how long its supposed to take? Sorry Im new to this whole thing.
Like 10

Teresa Constantine I have been really sad, after three months I'm only 3 kilograms down, but my jeans are definitely lose on me, I needed to go and buy a belt to keep them up. I don't understand, can someone explain it to me. How can you not loose weight in kilos but still lose a dress sizes?
Like 17

Stanley Miles
Seriously! This just proves that you've all been completely brainwashed. You're not even losing weight, yet you still bow down to this ridiculous fad. Bet you it was invented by the cauliflower farmers, and they paid Noakes a pretty penny. I suspect cauliflower sales have never been so good. Actually I was wrong, you are losers after all!
Like 1
View 527 more comments

THE CEO

Ring ring, ring ring, ring ring, ring ring, ring ring, ring ring, ring ring, ring ring, ring ring, ring ring, ring ring, ring ring, ring ring, ring ring, ring ring, ring ring, ring ring.

'This mailbox is full and cannot accept new messages.'

Trevor dropped the handset in frustration and stood watching it dangling from the base of the payphone. He was fucked. Royally, royally fucked.

Trevor needed to make another plan. He couldn't just idly watch his life collapsing around his ears. If only the hitman would get in touch, reassure him he wasn't being set up. The uncertainty was literally eating him up.

Trevor shuffled back down the street in the dark, dragging his feet along the pavement towards his office so he could fetch his car and go home, the still-dangling handset mocking him behind his back. He had a bag of Quality Street chocolates at home with his name on it. They were supposed to be for his great-aunt's birthday, but he would just have to buy her something else. Maybe a nice scarf.

BENJAMIN

Benjamin Di Rosi I just read your post on the Banting for Life Facebook page about Ginger Mary! I'm SO sorry, Lydia. You must be absolutely devastated. I know how much you loved that cat. I'm also sorry I've been scarce today, I know it's late, but I only just logged on and I hope you're still around to see this message. Things have been a little crazy on my side. Are you okay? If there is anything I can do, I hope you know that you only have to say the word and I'll be there for you.

> Lydia Steenberg Thank you so much, Benjamin. It's good to hear from you. Yes, I am devastated and crying as I write this. It was just so sudden. This morning when I went to work there she was, lying in the laundry basket. She was run over some time earlier today. I am finding it so hard to believe that she's really gone. I appreciate the support I've been getting from everyone on the page, and your support and kindness means a great deal to me.

Benjamin Di Rosi I know what a great cat she was. I can only begin to imagine how awful you're feeling. Although, I do think I can relate a small amount. The truth is, I've been having a pretty awful day myself.

> Lydia Steenberg Oh no, I'm sorry to hear you're having a rough time. Do you want to talk about it? I know talking about Ginger Mary in the group has really made me feel better, talking may do the same for you.

Benjamin Di Rosi Things at work are very stressful right now. I've been there for seven years and I've put so much effort and passion into it, but I'm not sure it's going to work out.

> Lydia Steenberg Oh I'm so sorry, Benjamin. It sounds like you work very hard, and take your job really seriously.

Benjamin Di Rosi There were rumours today that they're planning more cutbacks and retrenchments down the line, and if I'm being honest, I must say I'm concerned.

Lydia Steenberg Oh how awful. What is it that you do?

Benjamin Di Rosi I head up the sales department for a dental corporation. You wouldn't have heard of us. We supply dental equipment and cleaning products directly to the industry, dentists, orthodontists, that kind of thing.

Lydia Steenberg That sounds interesting. You sound very important and also very dedicated. I'm sure your family is very proud of you. And that company would be crazy not to keep you on.

Benjamin Di Rosi I hope so. It feels out of my control at this stage. But the real problem is all this stress – it's a big trigger for me. I'm permanently hungry and not making the best food choices. Over the last little while I've been putting all the weight I fought so hard to lose back on.

Lydia Steenberg Oh no, Benjamin. I totally understand what you're going through. Modern living is very stressful. Whenever I'm in that kind of situation, I always think, WWTND. I even had it engraved on a bracelet a while ago so I can look at it whenever I'm feeling weak. Just looking at it always makes me strong again. Although I did eat three Romany Creams with my tea tonight, but I think that's understandable under the circumstances.

Benjamin Di Rosi Of course it is! You poor thing. But what is WWTND? Is it the same as BPC? Cos I tried that and I must say, I didn't like it very much.

Lydia Steenberg lol, sorry, I'm not laughing at you ... it's not Bullet Proof Coffee (Yum, I love it, have you tried it with an egg broken into it? Maureen has a great recipe for it with her meal plans.) No, WWTND is What Would Tim Noakes Do?

Benjamin Di Rosi Ohhhh lol, yes that makes more sense. A raw egg in coffee! Yuck!

Lydia Steenberg It's nicer than it sounds. And if WWTND doesn't work for me, then I think WWMMEMPD.

Benjamin Di Rosi Wow, that's a long one, I'm not sure you'd be able to fit that on a bracelet. What does that mean?

Lydia Steenberg Ha ha ha, that's 'What Would Maureen's Marvellous ENDORSED Meal Plans Do.' ☺ Did you get in touch with her yet?

Benjamin Di Rosi No, but I will try do it tomorrow. I feel so much better after talking to you. Thank you.

Lydia Steenberg Thank you. It's nice talking to you too. You've cheered me up no end, I hope I've done the same for you?

Benjamin Di Rosi You really have. I was feeling so bleak and hopeless and having the most awful thoughts, and feeling constantly hungry, but I'm feeling better now, thank you. All right, I'd better get back to work, I'm still at the office and it's late, I need to just wrap up here, and then I can head home. Is it okay if I message you again in the morning?

Lydia Steenberg I'd like that. Just remember, WWTND. And also don't worry too much about work, you're an asset and they're lucky to have you. Chat tomorrow.

Benjamin Di Rosi Thank you again. And be strong, I'm sorry about Ginger Mary, am thinking of you and sending strength. My Silas sends condolences too. Night, night.

THE HIJACKERS

'… I love you more than Chicken Licken.'

…

'I love you more than Carling Black Label.'

…

'I love you more than my mama's pap and my Converse takkies, Zuki my baby,' Thabo crooned into the phone.

Papsak pulled the hood of his sweater over his face and groaned, then made vomiting noises.

'I promise I'll come visit you soon-soon, my baby.'

…

'No, I promise.'

…

'I'm not just saying it.'

…

'I'll come pick you up in my gusheshe.'

…

'I know you want me to come now, but I can't. I'm very busy working at work.'

….

'But I have to work, you want me to make money don't you? Then I can buy you anything you want.'

…

'Yes, even a cell phone.'

…

'Yes, of course with unlimited airtime.'

...

'No, I love you more.'

...

'No, I love you more.'

...

'No, *you* put down the phone first.'

...

'No, *you* put down first.'

...

'No, you.'

...

'No, you.'

...

'Okay, my sugar la-ding ding, we'll both put down together ... one, two, three...'

...

'I can also still hear you breathing.' Thabo burst out laughing.

Papsak grabbed the phone out of Thabo's hand and cut off the call.

'Hey, what did you do that for?' Thabo yelled.

'We've been driving around for hours now, it's late and I'm tired, and Uncle Mlungu is starting to smell. He's going to ruin the seats at the back of our gusheshe. When are we going to dump him so we can go home? Mama is going to be worried if I'm not home again tonight.'

'Okay, Paps, let's keep driving and see if we can't find somewhere deserted. How much more money have you got? We're running low on petrol.'

THE CO-AUTHORS

'Hello, Cyril speaking.'

'Cyril, it's Shaun Thomas.'

'Oh, hello Shaun. I'm so sorry to hear about the Prof.'

'Thanks, but I called because there's something I need to talk to you about.'

'Is everything okay?'

'I'm sorry to have to do this to you, but I think you ought to know. If I was in your position, I would want to know.'

'What? You're making me nervous, Shaun. Have you been drinking?'

'You know how you thought Xolisa was staying over at her sister's place last night, and a few times every week for the last month or so?'

'Yes?'

'She wasn't.'

'What on earth do you mean?'

'Don't be so naïve, Cyril.'

'What the hell are you talking about?'

'She was right about you, Cyril, you are an idiot.'

'Now you wait a damn...'

'Wake up and open your eyes. I've been fucking your wife behind your back for weeks.'

'You fucking a...'

But there was a beep, beep, beep, and Cyril was left with nothing but the dialing tone.

THE HIJACKERS

'Thabo, brother, look at this, I can't believe it!' Papsak shrieked.

'What? Did you find money for petrol?' Thabo asked, craning to see what Papsak had found in the cubbyhole of the gusheshe.

'No, something much, much better,' Papsak said, dangling a small bank bag that contained marijuana and a packet of Rizlas in front of Thabo's face. 'Lefty must have missed it.'

'Or forgotten it.'

'Maybe it was on his blind side.'

The two men roared with laughter, then fist-bumped.

'You drive, I'll roll,' Papsak said. 'Find us somewhere we can park.'

'But what about Uncle Mlungu?'

'He can't have any.'

THE COP

'Felicia, I can't sleep with you crying like that, and I really need to get some rest,' Bennie September said, patting his sobbing wife gently on the arm.

'I'm sorry, Bennie, but I just can't believe he's dead.' Felicia wiped her eyes on the sleeve of her nightie.

'Sweetie, I know it's sad that Professor Noakes has gone, but you didn't even know him.'

'Well, I feel like I know him, okay! He changed my life. Plus I once saw him at the coffee shop at Palmyra Junction, you know?'

'So you've said, about a billion times.'

'He looked so kind, nê, the way he was stirring his coffee.' Felicia started sobbing again. 'Promise me you'll catch the bastards who did this, Bennie! Swear to me!'

'I'm going to do my best, sweetie. But I can't do my job if I don't get any sleep.'

'Promise me!' Felicia sobbed. 'Cross your heart and hope to die.'

'Felicia, come now, I promise, I'll try my hardest.'

His wife blew her nose loudly, then sank back into her pillows, and heaved a few more sobs. Then sighed heavily, and a minute later her breathing slowly started to even out until she was snoring.

'Great!' Bennie sighed under his breath. How was he going to get to sleep now? He didn't sleep a wink last night because of the murder – and then the fucking hijacking and the missing body. He couldn't go another night without sleep – he'd be a mess tomorrow. God help him if he ever told his charming, dainty wife that she snored like a two-stroke chainsaw. He'd considered recording her on his cell phone one night and making her listen to the proof, but he'd always chickened out in the end. Here he was, a cop who dealt with some of the nastiest pieces of human shit this country managed to produce, and yet he was still too scared to tell his wife she snored.

How did she do that, he wondered? She could be awake one second, and fast asleep the next. It drove him nuts. Ooh. Nuts. He rubbed his stomach, then sat up, slipped his feet into his blue stokies and padded down to the kitchen. He stood staring into the fridge and rubbed his stomach again. He scooped up a handful of something green and sniffed at it. Ugh, kale.

Bennie shuffled into the garage, unlocked his car and felt under the passenger seat for the cardboard Pick 'n Pay box, just in case he'd left an uneaten donut behind by accident. Fat chance: the box was empty, not even crumbs left. He spotted a green jelly baby in the footwell of the car on the driver's side. Leaning in, he picked it up, wiped the fluff off of it and popped it in his mouth. Standards had dropped drastically.

'Don't turn around,' Trevor quavered. 'Don't look at me. Just keep drivin', mate.'

'What's wrong with your voice?' asked the taxi driver.

'It's my accent, it's cockney,' Trevor said.

'You're from a place called Cock?'

'No, it's … never mind. Look, they told me at the taxi rank that if I needed somefing taken care of, you're the man, innit?'

Trevor's voice wobbled. It had been bad enough, a white man wandering around a taxi rank late at night with a plastic bag full of cash, asking if there was someone who 'sorted out problems'. The taxi driver he had been directed to certainly looked the part. He was huge, with what looked like ritual scars on his face. Probably some prison gang thing.

'I can try to help you, brother. But you need to tell me more,' said the taxi driver.

'I 'ave the money 'ere, twenty up front, twenty later when it's all been taken care of, plus all the information I could get me 'ands on about this person, name, number and so on. The one that needs taking care of. But there's a small problem...' Trevor blurted out.

'What now?' The taxi driver looked over his shoulder again.

'Please keep your eyes on the road!' Trevor yipped, forgetting his accent.

The taxi driver rolled his eyes, then turned to face the front again. They were driving slowly down a deserted road near the airport. A lone pedestrian tried to wave them down, then shouted something insulting as they barrelled past.

'What problem?' the driver asked.

'I need this done urgently, sooner the better. But the bloke involved, 'e may not be so easy to track down. I 'aven't been able to get hold of him on his cell phone. And also, well, he's in the same industry as you.'

'He drives a taxi?'

'Not that industry, the other one.'

The taxi driver whistled.

'Also, er, this problem guy, 'e might be in prison. But you got connections inside, right?'

Trevor passed the man his plastic bag with a shaking hand. The driver used his knees to steer as he flipped through the notes.

'It's all there,' Trevor said. 'You'll get the rest when the thing has been done. With a small bonus if you do it within the next twenty-four hours. My pager number is written on a slip of paper with the cash. Once you find him and "take care" of him, call me from his phone. Then I'll know for sure you've done it. That make sense?'

There was a long silence, then: 'We have an agreement,' rumbled from the front.

The taxi driver dropped Trevor at the airport – International Departures. Then he drove back to Khayelitsha praying for forgiveness for his sins. The stupid white man thought he could hire any old taxi driver to kill someone, and all because of that terrible Dewani thing, when some tsotsi taxi drivers had murdered a poor sweet Indian girl on her honeymoon, giving good taxi drivers everywhere a bad name. So perhaps God would forgive him for taking the stupid racist mlungu's money. He'd nearly driven off the road when he'd seen the fat wad of R200 notes. But then he'd realised that Jesus was answering his prayers. He'd be able to get a new roof for Sis Sindiwe's crèche for the orphans. And maybe he and the others of the Tabernacle Gospel House of Prayer could take the children to the sea for the day, fill up their tummies with fish 'n chips. And with whatever was left over he could buy some textbooks for the prisoners' rehab programme he ran. He began to sing: 'Hallelujah, I thank you Lord for stupid white men…'

Trevor hired another taxi from outside International Departures, this time a metered sedan, to drive him back into town. If he'd had his passport with him, he would have jumped on the next plane going anywhere and disappeared forever.

Twenty minutes later, the taxi dropped Trevor off at his car on Green Point Main Road. He crossed the road, looking lovingly at his Merc.

His life had taken a horrible turn for the worse. He was officially a murderer, a double murderer. He wondered if this made him a serial killer.

But he hadn't had a choice in the matter, had he? If he didn't do something, he would definitely lose his job. And if he lost his job, he would have to give up the penthouse and the Merc. And then he'd definitely never get a girlfriend.

Everything would be okay now, surely? Paying hitmen to rub each other out couldn't be the worst thing, could it?

Trevor pressed the remote to unlock the Merc, then changed his mind and pressed the remote again to relock it. Then he walked into the twenty-four-hour KFC. His guilt and anxiety were chewing him up; he might as well return the favour.

THE FANS

Wednesday 11:32pm

THE BANTING FOR LIFE FACEBOOK PAGE

Herman De Laat
Hey everyone, I was just thinking how when you're Banting everything changes. We even need new sayings, anyone have any suggestions for a new saying to replace "The best thing since sliced bread"?

My attempt: "The best thing since bacon snacks".
Like 304

Annelize Van Tonder Best thing since biltong.
Like 24

Siyamthanda Sekota Best thing since psyllium husk. ☺
Like 2

Tina Zylstra Best thing since Tim Noakes. ☹
Like 1040

Anton Norris **How about the worst thing** since Tim Noakes! What a bunch of fatty fools you all are, taken in by a charllatan. Your lucky he's dead, otherwise he would have brought out another book in a years time to pick you're pockets again, about how carbs are the new salad or something like that!
Like 2

Herman De Laat Have some respect, you idiot!
Like 1098

Siyamthanda Sekota What's wrong with you, Norris, a great man has died, we're all in mourning.
Like 1698
View 1107 more comments

THE CEO

Trevor tossed and turned, but even though he was achingly tired in every single joint, muscle and bone, it wasn't the kind of tired that would let him sleep. It was three minutes past two, then fifteen minutes later it was only five minutes past two. He got up. There was no point lying there going mental doing ceiling duty.

He made himself a cup of warm milk, he'd seen that in the movies before, although in the movies nobody ever burned the pot and scalded three fingers.

Then he tried to go to sleep again. After a while, he got up and rifled through the medicine cabinet to see if there was anything that would help. He took three expired sleeping pills, got back into bed and stared at the ceiling for another forty minutes. Then he got up and took two Panados in case they'd do the trick and activate the sleeping pills. They didn't. Sleep was nowhere.

He watched a Ginsu knives commercial on e.tv, then surfed through the channels and watched the second half of one of the *Die Hard* movies. The whole time his mind raced, alternating between the fear of being caught, and the guilt of what he'd done. He might keep his job, but he was definitely going to hell now. One dead body was bad; two was unconscionable.

Trevor went to heat another cup of milk, but discovered he was all out. He'd put the carton back in the fridge with only an inch of milk left in it. It was one of the things he did that had annoyed the crap out of his ex-wife, and now he could see why. At least she had been able to divorce him and get away. She was the lucky one; he was stuck with himself forever.

He walked out of his apartment in his socks, pyjama bottoms and a t-shirt, and dragged his feet along the pavement all the way to the twenty-four-hour garage. When he got there and took a carton of milk to the till, he patted his pockets and realised he hadn't brought his wallet, just the fucking mute pager.

Trevor loped back to his apartment, the hems of his pyjama bottoms dragging along the ground. He left muddy footprints on the carpet in a trail from the front door all the way to his medicine cabinet, where he took another two sleeping pills, then back to the couch, where he flopped down, turned on the TV and watched the Ginsu knives commercial again and again, until it was time to go to work.

THE HIJACKERS

'Wake up, bra,' said Thabo, nudging Papsak, who was slumped to one side in the passenger seat, his jacket covering him like a blanket.

Papsak mumbled something and turned away from Thabo.

'You've got to get up.' Thabo slapped his friend, knocking the Supersport cap off his head.

Papsak grumbled and then pulled the car seat upright and rubbed his eyes. 'What happened?'

'It's morning, we must have passed out.'

The two men turned in their seats. Uncle Mlungu was still in the back seat with his seat belt on. He had his beanie and sunglasses on, and a half-smoked cigarette sticking out of blue lips. Both his arms were raised above his head, touching the roof of the car.

'No, man! Why didn't we get rid of him last night?' Thabo shouted. 'This is all your fault, Papsak! I told you we should have dumped him before we smoked all that stuff.'

Papsak shrugged. 'My mouth tastes like something died in it.' He climbed out the car to go pee against a nearby tree.

'Mine too. Hey Papsak, hurry up, look, there's nobody around, if we're quick we can dump him here now.' Thabo got out and opened the back door of the gusheshe, undoing Uncle Mlungu's seat belt. 'Tyhini, he weighs a ton, and he's all stiff now, I can't get him out. Come help me quickly.'

Papsak zipped up his fly, then ran to the other side of the car and climbed in the back seat next to Uncle.

'Push him!' Thabo shouted.

'I am pushing, but he's stiff like steel, he doesn't want to go anywhere,' Papsak yelled back, pushing hard at the other side of the dead body.

'It's his arms, they're getting stuck in the doorway, why are they up in the air like that? I can't get them out of the door,' Thabo said. 'Try pull his arms down, Papsak.'

'I can't, they're stuck in the air like this!' Papsak said, pulling down on Uncle Mlungu's right arm, practically hanging on it.

'Maybe if we roll him onto his side we can pull him out that way?' Thabo suggested, trying to push the body over on the back seat.

'I think Uncle is stuck to the seat,' Papsak said, leaning back and trying to heave the body over.

'Fok, somebody's coming,' Thabo hissed. 'Eish, it's more runners!'

Papsak pulled Uncle's beanie down over his face, knocking his sunglasses off, snapping the cigarette in half and sending it flying. They jumped into the front and sped off before the runners reached them.

'Shit, shit, shit!' Thabo smacked his palm against the steering wheel in frustration. 'What did you do to Uncle Mlungu last night, Papsak? Why are his arms stuck up in the air like that?'

'Don't you remember, Thabs? Last night we were pretending we were at Ratanga Junction. We put Uncle on the rollercoaster, remember? Everyone always puts their hands up on there.' Papsak burst out laughing at the memory. 'But I think Uncle Mlungu preferred the ice cream and candy floss.'

BENJAMIN

Thursday 7:49am

Benjamin Di Rosi Lydia, are you there? Lydia?

> **Lydia Steenberg** Hi, yes, I'm here. Just leaving for work. Morning.

Benjamin Di Rosi I'm sorry to write so early, but I needed to talk to somebody, and I didn't know who else to turn to.

> **Lydia Steenberg** Oh my goodness, what? Are you okay?

Benjamin Di Rosi Lydia, I've done something terrible, something horrific, something unforgivable.

> **Lydia Steenberg** Benjamin, you're scaring me now. Nothing is unforgivable, I'm sure whatever you did, you had good reasons for it.

Benjamin Di Rosi I did, I really did.

> **Lydia Steenberg** Trust me, whatever you've done can't be as bad as some of the things I've done in my life! It's not like you killed anyone or anything.

Benjamin Di Rosi Well, ummm...

> **Lydia Steenberg** Benjamin?!

Benjamin Di Rosi I'm worried if I tell you, you'll never talk to me again.

> **Lydia Steenberg** Listen, Benjamin, I think you may have put me on a pedestal; you think I'm this sweet innocent girl, but I've done bad things too. Everybody has some skeletons in their closet, or things they aren't proud of. I've been dishonest, I've lied to people.

Benjamin Di Rosi Lydia, I've hurt a lot of people! It's all
my fault, and it's chewing me up, I can't sleep and I crave carbs
all the time.

>Lydia Steenberg It's okay, Benjamin. Can I call you Ben? We all
>have our reasons for doing the things we do that hurt other people.
>We're only human. We're weak, lonely, flawed. You seem like a
>good person, you work hard, I can't believe you would have done
>anything awful on purpose. Maybe you just need a bit of sleep and
>to start eating properly again. I know if I eat carbs I really struggle.

Benjamin Di Rosi Yes maybe you're right...

>Lydia Steenberg Sometimes we have to do things that may not
>necessarily be considered the right thing to do, traditionally, but
>we all have our reasons ... we do what we have to do to make our
>lives better.

Benjamin Di Rosi You're right, you shouldn't listen to me,
I'm exhausted, I'm not making sense.

>Lydia Steenberg I really do have to get to work, but you need
>to know that everything is going to be okay. It will all work out in
>the end, and if it hasn't worked out yet, that just means it's not the
>end.

Benjamin Di Rosi Thank you, Lydia. You have no idea how
grateful I am to have you to talk to.

>Lydia Steenberg Me too. Feel better, chat later, Ben.

By the time Trevor saw Gunther walking through his office door, it was too late to fling himself out of the window. He was so tired, he felt like he'd been wading through treacle all morning. Gunther was the last thing he needed. He stood and reached for his jacket.

'Trevor, I've been trying to get hold of you,' Gunther said.

'You have?' Trevor started pulling his jacket on, realising half-way through that it was inside-out and not having the energy to fix it. 'I was just on my way out, important meeting with the sales team, this will have to wait!'

'I've left you at least five messages. Why haven't you returned any of my calls?'

'Really?' Trevor tried to sound surprised. 'Could we perhaps pick this up tomorrow? I'm running terribly late.' He glanced at his watch, realising too late that in his mushy-brain state he had forgotten to put the stupid thing on.

'We can't pick this up tomorrow or any other time. I need to speak to you right now. Sit down.' Gunther pointed to Trevor's guest chair, as if it were his own office.

As Trevor sat down slowly, he noticed that Gunther had decided to remain standing. He moved to stand, knowing that in the power politics of the boardroom, it was important never to be the lowest person in the room. If your adversary was standing, you should stand too, just to even the playing field. But seeing the stern look on Gunther's face, he realised he didn't have the energy for power politics anymore, and sagged back down in his seat. Here it comes, he thought.

'We have a problem, Trevor.' Gunther reached into his pocket and pulled out a plastic sachet.

'Have you seen this?' Gunther handed Trevor the packet.

'Sure,' Trevor said, turning it over in his hands. It was one of their products.

'Take a closer look.'

Trevor turned it over again, not quite sure what he was supposed to be looking for.

'Notice anything missing?' Gunther asked.

'I'm sorry, but no, I don't. Perhaps you should just tell me what's going on here, Gunther.'

'Well, if you look closely, you'll notice that our standard disclaimer is missing from this particular package.'

Trevor spun the packet around and examined the back, squinting so he could read the small print without his glasses on.

'If you could just confirm one fact for me, please. It is your responsibility to ultimately sign off on all packaging, is it not?' Gunther went on.

'You know it is, Gunther. You wrote my contract.'

'Well, our problem is that this product is missing the very important disclaimer that states that this product was made in a factory that uses nut products.'

Trevor took another look at the packet and felt his scrotum shrivel.

'I'm sure you'll agree with me that someone has to take responsibility for this gross error in judgement. The board had an emergency meeting last night, and I'm afraid we're going to have to let you go with immediate effect.'

'That's nuts.'

'I don't think it's nuts, and I resent your levity, Trevor. It's an incredibly serious matter. Do you realise we are going to have to recall the product? That's more than thirty thousand individual units. Plus all the ones we have in the warehouse at present will have to be reprocessed and repackaged. We'll also have to put out a public safety message through the press. Do you have any idea what this little error of yours is going to cost us, besides the damage that it's going to do to our corporate and brand image? It's a public relations disaster!' Gunther spat.

From where Trevor sat, he could see up the Chairman of the Board's nose. 'No, Gunther,' he said patiently, 'I mean it's literally a packet of assorted nuts! Of course it's made in a factory that uses nuts, because … well, because they're nuts.'

'Yes, we discussed that point in our board meeting at great length. However, we all agreed that this kind of egregious mistake could very well result in us being sued by some poor unsuspecting consumer who happens to have a nut allergy.'

'But Gunther, surely anyone with a nut allergy would know not to purchase, open and then eat what is clearly a bag of nuts?' Trevor stammered.

'Be that as it may, you've really left us no choice,' intoned Gunther. 'It's simply one misjudgement too many. The board is concerned that you may be having some form of mental breakdown, and that keeping you on puts the corporation at even further financial and legal risk. Our decision is final.'

Trevor nodded. Then he got to his feet and walked out of his office for the last time. Not caring that his jacket was still on inside-out, or that he was still wearing his pyjama bottoms from the night before.

THE EX-PUBLISHER

'Am I dead?' Frank mumbled as he swam to the surface of consciousness from the depths of what felt like hell.

His eyes were gummy and swollen, his mouth furry, and the smell … the smell was horrific. He sat up, wondering where he was, but the pain that seared through his head and his right hand was so severe, he had to lie back down again and re-close his eyes.

After a long minute, Frank forced himself to open his eyes again if only so that he could work out where he was; otherwise he would have kept them closed for the rest of eternity. He sat up once again, this time much more slowly and carefully. And it became horrifyingly apparent to him that he wasn't at home, but in some kind of cell. Three of the walls were concrete, and the fourth consisted of floor-to-ceiling metal bars.

He looked down at his right hand, which was throbbing. His fist had been wrapped in a dirty white bandage, and blood had seeped through in spots at his knuckles, and darkened to a muddy brown. He nursed the arm, holding his hand up by the elbow, so as not to allow his fist to touch any surfaces. The pain jabbed at him like a red-hot poker.

The cell had no external windows, so he had no clues as to the time of day or his location. It was lit by two fluorescent bulbs, one of which was dead, thankfully. Frank's scratchy eyes and porridge brain could only handle so much light. He smacked his lips together, after first having to tear them apart. Breathing deeply to keep his panic at bay didn't help; the smell of urine and vomit assaulted his nostrils.

Small flashes came back to him. The drunken night before last, and the resulting broken hand, punching the cardboard cutout in the bookstore before walking out on his job, the bar down the street, drinking, ranting, drinking: then nothing. His stomach burned, and he bent over the lidless toilet and vomited up stinging, hot, yellow bile.

The sound of his retching brought a policewoman to the bars of his cell.

'Oh good, you're alive,' the policewoman said. 'I'll call September.'

September? Frank thought. Shit, had he been passed out for three months?

THE EX-CEO

Trevor followed his feet down the green-carpeted passage and out of his office building for the last time. Earlier that morning he had somehow managed to put on his work shoes, and get them on the right feet, but he wasn't quite sure how he'd missed the whole pants thing.

When Trevor looked around, he found himself at the payphone again. He'd practically worn a trail in the pavement between it and his office. Muscle memory alone had gotten him there. He felt in the pockets of his plaid pyjama pants for his wallet, but his pockets were still empty except for that stupid, impotent pager, which stubbornly refused to show any messages.

Trevor slumped down on the ground next to the payphone and tried to work out his next move. He wondered where his first hitman was, and how much trouble he was in. Chances were high that the first hitman was the suspect the press had reported was in custody. It was the only thing that explained his radio silence. But that was yesterday; surely by now he would have ratted Trevor out? So why hadn't the cops come for him yet? Trevor wondered how much they'd had to torture the hitman to spill the beans. Or would just the insinuation of jumper leads on his gonads do the job? If somebody put jumper leads anywhere near his nuts, he'd sing like a canary.

But maybe he was being paranoid, Trevor told himself for the thousandth time. What if the first hitman had offed the Prof as planned, and then done a runner straight out the country? What if he was happily settled somewhere in Cancun right this second, drinking a margarita and getting a lap dance, and the reason he hadn't answered any of Trevor's calls was because he didn't have roaming on his cell phone?

But the same old questions kept circling the drain that was Trevor's brain. Why hadn't he called for the rest of the money? Why do the job and then skip town without the remaining cash? Maybe the hitman had just been in the bath. For the last two days.

Trevor looked up as someone walked past in a blur and dropped a five-rand coin in his lap. No surprises there; he was sitting on the pavement next to a public phone, unshaven, in his now ragged and muddy-bottomed pyjama pants, businessman's shoes and an inside-out jacket, mumbling to himself.

Trevor spun the coin in his fingers, then stood and fed it into the phone and dialled the first hitman's number one more time. A number now so engrained in his brain he'd never forget it.

The phone rang and rang and rang. Again.

THE HIJACKERS

'This phone is making me crazy. Between you calling, calling, calling every babe in Khayelitsha and it ringing and ringing and ringing all night and all day ever since you got it,' said Papsak, rubbing his eyes. 'You must just turn it off before it makes me lose my mind.'

'I told you a thousand times, I can't turn it off,' Thabo said. 'If I turn it off, then when I turn it back on again, we'll have to put in a password to use Uncle Mlungu's free minutes, and I don't have his password. Do you know Uncle's password, hey? Do you?'

'Maybe Uncle Mlungu's password is "stinks like shit", or "going rotten".' Papsak turned up his nose and looked daggers over his shoulder at the offending corpse.

The phone stopped ringing. A minute later, it started up again.

'So, what are you going to do about it?' Papsak asked, nodding at the phone buzzing around in the gusheshe's consol.

'Just ignore it. We have more important problems.'

'I know! That's what I've been trying to say! We've been driving around forever, Thabo. Everywhere I say we must dump Uncle, you don't like it. Too light, too dark, too close to town, too close to people running. When is this all going to be over? I just want to go home and sleep.'

'We have a plan, Papsak, let's stick to it. We're going to drive around here and find a quiet spot, and then toss Uncle Mlungu in the sand dunes, remember? I think this will be perfect for us.'

'I hope so. I don't know why there are always so many people all the time in all the places where we want to dump Uncle. I'm tired, I want to go home,' Papsak whined.

'It's the beach, Papsak, we should have known there would be people here.'

'Why aren't they at work? And now what?'

'We just carry on driving around carefully till we find the right place. I know there will be one. And we don't break any laws, so the cops don't pull us over,' Thabo said. 'Everything will be fine, you'll see.'

Papsak didn't seem convinced. He pulled a face, then wound down his window and waved the fresh air in with his hand. 'Shew, Uncle Mlungu, sies man!'

THE FANS

THE BANTING FOR LIFE FACEBOOK PAGE

Lydia Steenberg
Hey everyone, this is one of my favourite Banting recipes, so I thought I'd share it with you all. I do find that on those cold mornings especially I miss oats. So here's one of the recipes I received with one of Maureen's Marvellous ENDORSED meal plans. I hope she doesn't mind me posting it here on the page, but I absolutely love it, so I wanted to share it. Just about every day I thank my lucky stars that I came across Maureen. Here it is:

Banting Porridge
A Tim Noakes ENDORSED recipe, created by Maureen Ewehout
- 2 tablespoons cashews
- 2 tablespoons almonds
- 2 tablespoons pecans
- 2 tablespoons walnuts
- 1 tablespoon sesame seeds
- 1 tablespoon pumpkin seeds
- 1 tablespoon chia seeds
- 100ml coconut milk or full cream milk
- A pinch of cinnamon
Place the nuts in a large bowl and sprinkle a little salt over them. Fill the bowl with water so the nuts are covered. Soak overnight. Then in the morning, drain the nuts and rinse 2 or 3 times until the water runs clear. Blend the nut mixture with coconut milk and cinnamon. Microwave for 30 seconds. Serve with strawberries and love, from Maureen and Tim Noakes too (RIP).
Like 243
View 27 more comments

THE HIJACKERS

Thursday 9:42am

The phone in the middle consol of the car started ringing again, making Papsak jump. 'Who is this, always looking for dead Uncle Mlungu?' he complained. 'And always the same number calling, every time.'

'Maybe it's his wife? She probably wants his body back so they can bury him.'

'What if it's the police?' Papsak asked, wide-eyed.

'I don't think it's the police. They have big computers that can track phones. If it was the police, they would have already found us and put us in jail.'

'Maybe you must just answer it next time it rings, and tell whoever is calling that Uncle Mlungu is dead and gone and they must stop phoning now.'

'Wait, you've given me an idea, Paps.' Thabo grabbed him by the sleeve of his jacket. 'Do you think whoever keeps phoning him would pay to get the body back?'

'What, like money?'

'Yes. We could get rid of the body for once and for all, and make some money at the same time.'

'Maybe. How much do you think we could get for Uncle?' Papsak asked.

'I don't know, what's a dead mlungu worth?'

'I don't know, about five thousand maybe?'

'What about a famous dead mlungu?'.

'Twelve thousand?'

'I'm thinking maybe even fifteen.'

'You think we could get fifteen thousand large for Uncle Mlungu, even though he's starting to smell like bad fish, or Brother Philemon from church?' Papsak asked.

'Maybe.'

'It's good that it's a lot of money. We will have to use some of it to re-cover the back seat of the gusheshe.'

Thabo nodded.

'Okay, so what do we do now? Do you want to phone that number that keeps calling so we can talk to them?'

'No, let's not waste airtime or battery.'

'We could always send a "please call me".'

Thabo looked down at the cell phone. 'We can't, the call isn't coming from a cell phone. We just wait for it to ring again.'

'What if it doesn't?'

'It will.'

THE CO-AUTHORS

'Chef!' The waiter came into the kitchen carrying a full plate of Italian roasted chicken with seasonal salad and cauli-mash.

'Is there a problem with the chicken?' Marco asked. The diner had taken one bite out of the chicken leg. Nothing else had been touched.

'No, it's not the chicken. The gentleman at table five wants to know if it comes with chips.'

Marco sighed. 'This restaurant is called the Banting Bistro. Did he not see the sign, or read the menu?'

'What should I tell him?' the waiter asked, looking bored.

'Take it back and ask if he'd like some asparagus chips instead.'

Marco peered through the hatch and watched the waiter walk back through the restaurant carrying the plate. There were only two tables occupied in the restaurant, and they'd been seated too far apart, so the place looked stark and felt very quiet. Marco turned up the music and made a mental note to remind the waiters to seat customers closer together. It helped create more of an ambience. Marco watched the waiter bend down to speak to the customer, a man in his fifties with a greying beard, accompanied by a woman with short grey hair, who was eating the cauli-risotto and artichoke hearts.

The waiter returned to the kitchen, still carrying the plate on his palm.

'He says if you won't make him chips, he's going down the street to McDonalds.'

'Oh fuck it,' Marco said, opening the deep freezer and pulling out a bag of McCain's rustic-cut frozen chips. 'Tell him they'll be out in a minute.'

THE EX-PUBLISHER

'… and you're sure you don't want a lawyer?' Detective September asked.

'Do you think I need one?' Frank rasped.

'If you haven't done anything wrong, then I don't see why.'

'To be honest, I don't remember very much about last night.' Frank licked his chapped lips and downed the paper cup of tepid water the detective had brought him.

'What about the night before that?' the cop asked. 'How much of that do you remember?'

'Why am I here?' Frank asked. 'I have the most vile fucking hangover of my life.'

'Mr Collins, are you aware that Professor Tim Noakes was murdered two nights ago in his home in Constantia?'

Frank couldn't help bristling at Noakes's name. 'Call me Frank,' he said. 'Of course I know, it was all over the news yesterday.'

'Okay, Frank, and where were you two nights ago, if you don't mind me asking?'

'I do mind you asking, actually!' Frank shot back.

'Why? If you don't have anything to hide, this should all be over within the hour, and you'll be home in time for an afternoon nap. You look like you need one.'

'Two nights ago I was at home. Alone. As usual. Okay? You happy now?'

'Not really, Frank. That's not what you told everyone in the Slug and Cactus last night, as well as the two policemen who arrested you.'

'You've got to be fucking kidding me. I would have told you I was

Dolly Parton last night and believed it myself. I was out of my fucking head!'

'Is it not true, Frank, that you believe Professor Noakes is the reason your career fell apart?' the detective asked, reading from his scribbled notes.

'Sure, but that doesn't mean I did him in. You've got zero proof.'

'Weeeelll, that's not strictly true, Frank,' said Detective September, his moustache twitching with excitement, threatening to dislodge a few crumbs. 'There's the small matter of the confession you kept making last night.'

Frank looked at him, dumbfounded.

'We have twelve eye-witnesses, or should I say ear-witnesses, who heard you say that you punched Tim Noakes in the face numerous times "until he fell over". I believe those were your exact words.'

'I did, but not like that! It was a cardboard cutout that I punched. As anyone at the bookshop where I work … worked,' Frank corrected himself, 'will tell you.'

The detective referred to his notes again. 'You also stated numerous times that you were glad he was dead. Plus there's also the state of your hand to consider,' September said. 'Your knuckles are shredded. We had a nurse look at you when they brought you in last night, and we suspect some of the bones in your hands are broken, Frank. You clearly hit something very hard. What are we supposed to think?'

'I punched a wall a couple of times, Detective. A fucking wall! That wasn't illegal last time I looked. Neither is being glad somebody is dead. I think maybe you'd better get me that lawyer now.'

'Frank…' Detective September began.

'Mr Collins to you, if you don't mind,' Frank grumbled. 'And I'd like another cup of water, and some Panado please. My brain feels three sizes too big for my fucking skull.'

THE CO-AUTHORS

'Oh God, please don't tell me you're on TripAdvisor again?'

'Look at these wankers, Chris. They've given my sun-dried tomato and ham cauli-pizza two stars. TWO STARS! That's my nonna's sun-dried tomato recipe. How dare they? "Rubbery!" they said! People have been making them like this in Italy for generations. These idiots wouldn't know a decent, properly cured sun-dried tomato if it jumped up and bit them in the face.'

'Honey, you're not writing a response, are you?' Chris said, putting on his glasses and leaning over Marco's shoulder to get a closer look at what he was bashing out on the poor, innocent keyboard.

'Oh, and guess where they're from? You get two guesses; no actually you only get one guess! They could only be from America!' Marco ranted.

'Marco,' Chris said gently, 'we've talked about this before, sweetheart. Step away from the keyboard right now. Remember, we agreed, we do not respond to trolls on the internet, particularly the ones on TripAdvisor.'

Marco stopped typing, looked at Chris, then took a deep breath and pushed the laptop away.

'I know … you're right,' Marco said. Then after a pause, 'Chris, do you think things would have been different if I'd gone on *MasterChef* instead?'

Chris sighed. 'Like I say every single time we have this conversation, of course they would have been different, but there are no guarantees that they would have been any better, my love.'

'I don't know if this is what I really want,' said Marco, knuckling his eyes.

'Why would you say that? You have your new book coming out in a few months, Noakes is out of the way so only your name will go on it, and you owe Shaun and Xolisa nothing. And Shireen, well, she's all the way up in Joburg, and everyone knows she's batshit crazy. So you don't have to share the limelight with anyone any more. You'll be a household name by the end of the year. Then the restaurant will pick up, and forget being a contestant on *MasterChef*, they'll be begging you to *judge* it.'

'I know ... I know. It's just I've given up so much to be here, but where has it gotten me? My restaurant is two Banting breakfasts away from closing down, my publisher airbrushed my author photo so much I look like a Kardashian, and now some tool on TripAdvisor says the chef at the Banting Bistro has two left hands. This isn't what I trained in Italy for seven years for. My whole life is food. Do you have any idea how difficult it is for me to make the kind of food I love, and the kind of food I'm proud of, living like this? I think I've made a terrible mistake.'

'Why would you say that? You're excited about the new book, aren't you?'

'You know I am. But honestly, Noakes wrote it. He's the household name. This is his work. I'm mostly just riding on his coat-tails. Of course I believe in what he's doing, sugar kills, and processed foods and carbs are the devil, we need to eat fresh homemade food, blah blah blah, but I miss making pasta and ciabatta and gnocchi, and ... and proper pizza, not cauli-pizza! My nonna lived to be ninety-seven, and she ate pasta every day of her life. Fresh, home-cooked pasta, made with love and no GMOs.'

'Come on, now you're being dramatic. Everything you cook you make with love. What's all this really about?'

'What if I'm not cut out for this lifestyle under a spotlight, Chris? I can't be seen out in public eating as much as a macaroon. I stress when

I put on a kilo. You know me, I'm a big guy naturally. What kind of Banting guru is twenty kilos overweight?'

'You know I prefer it when you're heavier, right? You're my bear. I don't like it when you're too skinny,' Chris said. 'You're perfect just the way you are.'

'I know, but that's because you love me. Out there I'll be a laughing stock.'

'Fuck out there, who cares about out there?' Chris said, waving him off. 'Look Marco, I love you and I'm behind you whatever you decide to do, but you need to decide now. Noakes is gone, so either you take this opportunity to reinvent yourself, bring out his book and make yourself famous off the back of it. Or go the other way, can it all, and find your own path, open an alphabetti spaghetti restaurant for all I care. But whatever you do, don't take all your shit out on those poor ignorant fuckers on TripAdvisor.'

THE BANTING FOR LIFE FACEBOOK PAGE

Nicky Page
Hello fellow Banting friends, I've struggled with my weight just about my entire life. I'm insulin resistant, with metabolic disorder, or what they term type two diabetes, which I manage with pills and exercise. I've managed to lose twenty kilograms over the last fifteen years, simply by watching what I eat fastidiously, and exercising at least three or four times a week. So my weight loss has been slow but consistent, which I'm proud of.

I found that eating carefully and running (I'm up to 5km, whooohoo) is enough to keep my weight steady, but I need to work really, really hard to chip off a couple of kilos in a year over and above that.

Seeing everyone's incredible success here on this page is one of the reasons that I decided to start Banting, and I'm in week three now.

I may not have picked the best time to start Banting, I'm overseas right now on a writer's retreat, writing a novel, and internationally they're not as Bant-friendly as they are in South Africa, but I'm giving it a try. Week one was difficult, I could feel myself coming off my carb addiction, and I lost two kilograms. Week two I felt quite hungry but I think my brain was just adjusting, and now at the beginning of week three, I feel like I may have actually put on weight, which is a bit devastating. There's no scale where I am out here in the middle of nowhere, but I'm going to keep on trucking. I want to thank all of you on this page for inspiring me with your words and pictures to give this thing a good bash. I see people on this page losing weight from the very first second, and I do wonder how long it will be before I start to see something shift?
Like 347

Maureen Ewehout well done for taking this first step towards changing your life, you can be very proud of yourself **Nicky Page**. Everyone has a different body and different metabolic issues. I create and sell individualised meal plans that have been ENDORSED by the late, great Tim Noakes, please DM me if

you'd like to chat about finding some personalised solutions tailormade for you.
Like 47

Nandi Gwashe Nicky, congratulations on starting your banting journey, you won't regret it. For me it took two months before the weight started to drop off, persevere and keep shifting your plan to see what works best for you. Stay with us.
Like 43

Nicky Viljoen Hi Nicky, some women struggle with diary, you might want to consider cutting down on your diary intake and seeing if that makes any difference. Good luck on your journey.
Like 65

Jeremy Dickinson Nicky, you'll kill yrself, please talk to yr doctor about this befor you carry on. I've seen peopole on this diet suffering from dangerously high cholesterol, kidney failure, weakening liver function. Don't add more sicknesses to list.
Like 0

Gary Biederasted I lost 7 kilos in my first week and another five in my second week. Love this way of life!!
Like 31
View 72 more comments

Cyril waited till Xolisa had left for the gym. Then he sat down at her laptop, used her password ('hammercurls x72') to gain access to her email account, and began scrolling.

In a folder marked 'Authors', he found what he was looking for. He clicked on an email from Shaun from a few weeks ago and scanned the thread of messages, his chest tightening as he read.

When he finally reached the bottom of the thread, he thought for a moment. Then he clicked on 'Forward', and selected Xolisa's entire address book. He checked to ensure that addresses for Tim Noakes and every board member of the Noakes Foundation, all the other authors, their publisher, and everyone they knew in family, business, the media and leisure were included.

Then he fumbled on the desk for the newspaper, searched the front page, and added the email address of the lead detective on the Noakes case. He hovered his mouse over the send button, took a deep breath and went for it.

FROM: Xolisabodyconstruct@gmail.com
SUBJECT: FWD: Your'e so sexy
DATE: Today at 4:21pm

Begin forwarded message:

From: "Shaun Thomas" <shaunthomas@plethora.co.za>
Date: 15 May 2015 at 11:36:18 AM SAST
To: "Xolisa Phillips" <Xolisabodyconstruct@gmail.com>
Subject: Your'e so sexy

Hi gorgeous, what you doing tomorrow night, do you want to come over?

From: "Xolisa Phillips" <Xolisabodyconstruct@gmail.com>
Date: 15 May 2015 at 11:54:37 AM SAST
To: "Shaun Thomas" <shaunthomas@plethora.co.za>
Subject: Re: Your'e so sexy

I want to, but what will I tell Cyril?

From: "Shaun Thomas" <shaunthomas@plethora.co.za>
Date: 15 May 2015 at 12:03:45 PM SAST
To: "Xolisa Phillips" <Xolisabodyconstruct@gmail.com>
Subject: Re: Your'e so sexy

Tell him youv'e got something on, there must be some function that you can pretend your going to. What grand opening or debate is the prof headlining at tomorrow night? You could just say your going to that.

From: "Xolisa Phillips" <Xolisabodyconstruct@gmail.com>
Date: 15 May 2015 at 12:07:02 PM SAST
To: "Shaun Thomas" <shaunthomas@plethora.co.za>
Subject: Re: Your'e so sexy

You're not kidding, that guy would go to the opening of an envelope if it had his name on it.

From: "Shaun Thomas" <shaunthomas@plethora.co.za>
Date: 15 May 2015 at 12:13:04 PM SAST
To: "Xolisa Phillips" <Xolisabodyconstruct@gmail.com>
Subject: Re: Your'e so sexy

Your so cute when you get angry. Wait, I remember the profs going to the opening of the National Gallery art thing tomorrow night, hes' the keynote speaker. Why do'nt you tell that wet blanket husband of yours thats where your going, and then come here and let a real man show you how its' done?

From: "Xolisa Phillips" <Xolisabodyconstruct@gmail.com>
Date: 15 May 2015 at 12:21:34 PM SAST
To: "Shaun Thomas" <shaunthomas@plethora.co.za>
Subject: Re: Your'e so sexy

What does the National Gallery and some art exhibition have to do with Banting anyway? Other than the fact that they're all so bloated with their own self-importance. I swear the prof drives me insane. Sometimes I just want to wrap my fingers around that leathery neck of his and squeeze till he shuts the fuck up.

From: "Shaun Thomas" <shaunthomas@plethora.co.za>
Date: 15 May 2015 at 12:30:19 PM SAST
To: "Xolisa Phillips" <Xolisabodyconstruct@gmail.com>
Subject: Re: Your'e so sexy

Hey I know, you leave Cyril, and Ill kill the Prof, and then you and I can become the new face of Banting. Fame and fortune at last.

From: "Xolisa Phillips" <Xolisabodyconstruct@gmail.com>
Date: 15 May 2015 at 12:35:29 PM SAST
To: "Shaun Thomas" <shaunthomas@plethora.co.za>
Subject: Re: Your'e so sexy

Ha, but what about Marco and Shireen?

From: "Shaun Thomas" <shaunthomas@plethora.co.za>
Date: 15 May 2015 at 12:40:12 PM SAST
To: "Xolisa Phillips" <Xolisabodyconstruct@gmail.com>
Subject: Re: Your'e so sexy

Marco Shmarco. Have you seen how badly old fattys' restaurant is doing?
That write-up in the paper last week was a shocker. He could no sooner fly
to the moon than front Banting for the public. He ate a flipping paste de
nata when we were at Vida last week, he's lucky there was'nt a journalist
or camera in sight. And Shireen is a dingbat.

From: "Xolisa Phillips" <Xolisabodyconstruct@gmail.com>
Date: 15 May 2015 at 12:48:51 PM SAST
To: "Shaun Thomas" <shaunthomas@plethora.co.za>
Subject: Re: Your'e so sexy

Ha, I know. Do you think he even noticed that they photoshopped half
of him out of those author photos? It's hilarious. How to lose thirty kilos
fast. As for Shireen, take away the nails and the hair, and she'd collapse.
Seriously, is there anything else holding her together?

From: "Shaun Thomas" <shaunthomas@plethora.co.za>
Date: 15 May 2015 at 12:57:38 PM SAST
To: "Xolisa Phillips" <Xolisabodyconstruct@gmail.com>
Subject: Re: Your'e so sexy

So what do you say about tomorrow night, is it a hot, dirty, sexy date? You know Id' do anything for you and your hot abs', baby...

From: "Xolisa Phillips" <Xolisabodyconstruct@gmail.com>
Date: 15 May 2015 at 1:02:19 PM SAST
To: "Shaun Thomas" <shaunthomas@plethora.co.za>
Subject: Re: Your'e so sexy

Awww, you'd kill Noakes for me? That's what I love about you, you're a man of action. That's so sexy. I'll meet you at your place so we can finesse our murder plans. I'll tell Cyril I'm going to that function, and I'll only be home really late.

From: "Shaun Thomas" <shaunthomas@plethora.co.za>
Date: 15 May 2015 at 1:07:59 PM SAST
To: "Xolisa Phillips" <Xolisabodyconstruct@gmail.com>
Subject: Re: Your'e so sexy

When I said there were things' I wanted to do for you, I kind of meant oral sex not murdering the prof, but we can talk about it. 😈
Ill pick up a bottle of champain on my way home. Xxx can't wait.

THE HIJACKERS

Ring ring, ring ring.

Thabo started, and Papsak went from fast asleep, his head leaning against the window, to wide awake and sitting up straight in one-third of a second. They both lunged for the ringing phone at the same time. But Thabo got to it a split second before Papsak.

'Hello,' he said cautiously.

'Hello?' Trevor said. ''Ello,' he tried again, remembering the cockney accent.

'Who is this?'

'Who is this?'

'Why are you calling Umlungu so many times?' Thabo shouted. 'He's dead, you can't speak to him.'

'Oh, it's you, er, Mr Driver?' Trevor's voice trembled with hope. If his second hitman was answering his first hitman's phone it could only mean he must have done the job. Relief washed over him. If hitman number one was dead, Trevor was in the clear, good to go, free as a bird.

'So he's dead, then?' Trevor asked. 'Definitely dead? White guy, tall, in his early sixties?'

'Dead dead,' Thabo said, wrinkling his nose and looking over his shoulder at Uncle Mlungu, who was in the process of decomposing in the back seat. 'That's why I'm using his phone. He has a lot of airtime left.'

'Oh thank God,' Trevor lapsed back into his real voice for a moment. 'So you must want the money now?'

'Yes please, I want the money. Fifteen thousand bucks.'

'Fifteen thousand?' Trevor asked.

'Yes. Fifteen thousand for the dead mlungu. That's my final offer.'

'Tell him you want it in cash,' Papsak whispered.

'I want it in cash.'

'In a bag,' Papsak whispered.

'In a bag.'

'No police,' Papsak whispered.

'No police,' Thabo said.

'And bring us another cell phone too, for me,' Papsak added. 'An Apple iPhone.'

Thabo hit Papsak on the shoulder.

'Meet me with the cash in the parking lot at the sand dunes there by the public toilet at Strandfontein beach midnight tonight,' said Thabo. 'And no funny business, or I'll shoot you.'

'I'll be there,' Trevor said. 'Will you be in a taxi?'

'No,' Thabo announced with pride, 'I've got a car now. It's a BMW.'

THE EX-CEO

The phone went dead and Trevor stood for a moment staring at the handset in his shaking hand. His second hitman was clearly better at his job than the first one he'd hired. And as an added bonus, he was giving Trevor a discount. He wasn't sure why he was getting five grand off their agreed price – he hadn't realised it was negotiable, but he wasn't about to point out an error in his favour.

Maybe the taxi-driver-cum-hitman was hoping for a referral, or repeat business? But that was never going to happen. He was done with this business. Never again, now that his tracks were covered. At last he could breathe, and try to get on with his life. Lydia was right; everybody did bad things at some point in their life, the trick was to learn from them and not repeat the mistakes. Or crimes, in his case. Now that he was free and clear of this whole mess, he could start looking for a new job and try to pick up the pieces of his life, all with fewer carbs. He would try to be a better person going forward, right his wrongs, do more charity work maybe.

All he had to do now was fetch the money from his safe at home to pay this guy, and then make his way out to Strandfontein in time for the drop-off later. Maybe he'd stop off for some slap chips and a piece of cake somewhere along the way. One last hurrah before he paid off the second hitman and got back on the carb-free, sugar-free, contraband-free and criminal conspiracy-free wagon.

THE WIDOW

Maureen Ewehout Hello Benjamin, my name is Maureen, and I am in the same Banting Facebook Group as you, Banting for Life. My friend and client Lydia Steenberg suggested I write to you, as she thought you could use my help. You see I am the creator of the Tim Noakes ENDORSED Marvellous Meal Plans, which I sell to help people like yourselves better manage and maximise the remarkable Banting way of life. These plans come with full shopping lists, plus I'm always on hand twenty-four hours a day (just about) to help you with any problems or queries you may have.

With my ENDORSED meal plans, living well and being the person you strive to be has never been easier.

I hope you don't mind me friending you on Facebook and messaging you directly like this, but I would really love to help you on your journey, it is what I do best.

If you are interested, perhaps you'd like to meet, say at the Mugg & Bean in Cavendish whenever it suits you and at your earliest convenience? Then I can assess your needs and come up with a brilliant ENDORSED plan that suits you perfectly!

I really hope to hear from you soon.

Maureen Ewehout
Creator of the official Tim Noakes ENDORSED Marvellous Meal Plans.

THE FANS

THE BANTING FOR LIFE FACEBOOK PAGE

Nizreen Sooliman 😖 feeling sick
Hi my name is Nizreen, and I am a Banter. I just ate a Whopper with fries and a coke!!
Like 72

Cliffy Oosthuizen No, your not a banter, that is rubbish. You don't deserve to say you're a banter!!! Epic Fail Nizreen! Serves you wright that you feel sick now. Get off this page if your' not taking it seriously. It's called the Banting For Life page, not the Banting 4 Sometimes When You Feel Like It page!
Like 1

Rochelle Simmons Don't be such a dipshit Cliffy. Everyone is human even alcoholics fall off the bandwagon every now and then. Nizreen, it's okay, pick yourself up, dust yourself off and start all over again tomorrow.
Like 53

Maureen Ewehout Nizreen, I'm here to tell you that you can do this. We all stumble and make mistakes. Please DM me if you want to talk about it. Don't let this wobble send you off track, okay?
Like 7

Cliffy Oosthuizen – no **Rochelle Simmons** – what do you want me to do, say that's okay and you can eat it whenever you want. it's not like that if she wants to poison herself that's fine, but I won't say it's okay and blow smoke up her ass. That stuff is rotten and I don't even want to see it on this page. What if someone sees what she posted, and just hearing about it makes them fall off the wagon too. It's irresponsible! Nizreen, if you're not in it to win it you shouldn't be Banting. That's all.
Like 12

Lisa Leib I had macaroni and cheese tonight, if that makes you feel any better, Nizreen. Misery loves company. We went to my outlaws for supper, and

my cow of a monster-in-law made mac & cheese, even though she knows I'm on LCHF. I'm sure she does it on purpose, she's such a cow, bet she's laughing now. And my husband loved it, ate it all up – he always says how much he loves her cooking. There was a salad but it wasn't enough and I was starving after a long day at work, so I had some. My tummy is paying for it now. She said she made it cos she knows how much the kids love it. Jaaa right! Also, Cliffy, you're a tonsil. We're all only human.
Like 39

Ashwin Naidoo I think Cliffy is right, she should be ashamed of herself, feel so bad that she doesn't transgress again!
Like 1

Rochelle Simmons transgress? What are you, the banting police?????
Like 18
View 134 more comments

THE EX-CEO

Trevor cruised into the designated drop-off point just before nine. It wasn't like he had anything else to do. He was operating on pure adrenalin (also the sugar rush from the slap chips and cake). Thoughts whirled in his head. What if the cops were doing a sting operation, and as soon as he handed over the money, they burst out from behind a bush and arrested him?

He knew it was unlikely: why would the taxi driver double-cross him? It didn't make business sense. Plus he'd answered the first hitman's cell phone. He would only be able to do that if he'd managed to take out the first hitman. Unless, Trevor thought, they were all working together, but how? That didn't seem possible. His brain felt addled, incapable of following a single thought through to its logical conclusion. He blamed it on the sugar.

Trevor parked in the lee of the dunes; it was dark and there were no other cars, only the dunes rising up on either side of the road, and the hulking shape of the battered building housing the public toilets. He trekked up over the shifting sand to find the highest vantage point and get the lay of the land. His still-pyjama'ed legs sunk in deep at every step, exhaustion creeping further into his bones. As he reached the top of the dune, one leg sank into the sand past his knee and when he pulled it out again, he noticed he no longer had a shoe on the end of that foot.

Trevor slumped down at the top of the dune with the deep, dark, cold stretch of the ocean before him, and pulled his jacket closer around him as he scoped out his surroundings. He couldn't see any large SWAT operations being set up: no lights, no cars and not a person in sight.

After what felt like ages shivering on the dune, the only moving thing Trevor had noticed was a very old maroon BMW, which had been circling the area. Was that his second hitman?

At eleven, Trevor began the trek back down the dunes to his car, then left the parking lot. He spent an hour driving around within a five-kilometer radius of the drop-off point, on high alert, his eyes peeled for anything out of the ordinary.

THE HIJACKERS

'So you know what to do, hey Papsak? You go up onto that dune, and watch down here. If you see cops coming, whistle, then I'll run into those dunes. You run in the opposite direction, and I'll see you at home,' Thabo said.

Papsak nodded, but his eyes were wide. They hugged hard and slapped each other on the back.

'Hamba kahle, Uncle Mlungu,' Papsak said to the body perched on the back seat; then he turned and scampered off into the dunes.

Thabo turned as a white Merc driven by a bald mlungu pulled into the parking lot. It crunched to a halt beside him, and the man rolled down his window.

"Ello,' the man said, in the funny accent Thabo recognised from their earlier phone call.

'Do you have the money?' he asked in his most threatening voice.

"ow do I know you're not with the p'lice?' the man said. He seemed very nervous, and he smelt like slap chips.

'I've been driving around with a dead body in my car for the last two days! How do I know *you're* not with the police?' Thabo said.

'I'm not the rozzers, I swear on my loife,' the man said. 'I'm goin' to get out the car now, I'm not armed.' He climbed slowly and wearily out of his car with both hands in the air, a Shoprite bag dangling from one thumb. Thabo noticed he was unshaven, wearing an inside-out suit jacket, a shirt and tie and a pair of pyjama bottoms. He had on only one shoe, and his sock was covered in sand. This man looked like a crazy person, not a policeman.

'That's 'im. I can't believe it! You really got 'im!' The bald man peered into the back of the gusheshe.

'I told you I had the body,' Thabo said.

The man handed Thabo the shopping bag, which was packed with one-hundred-rand notes. 'It's all there, I promise.'

Thabo shoved the bag inside his jacket, then opened his back door. Reaching in, he clasped Uncle Mlungu around the chest and dragged his body out of the car. Uncle's arms had thankfully dropped back down by now, and he was less stiff than he had been before, but more smelly. He was also even heavier than Thabo had expected, and he began to sweat with the effort of heaving the two-days dead body.

'Quickly, open your back door,' Thabo instructed the bald man, his nose wrinkled in disgust.

'What are you doing?' the bald man asked, his voice shocked, his accent suddenly gone.

'I'm giving you the body you paid for. Watch out, he's heavy.'

'I don't want the body!' the bald man gasped in horror.

'You paid for him, you must take the mlungu,' Thabo insisted, equally horrified at the thought of being stuck with Uncle. 'Open your door!'

The bald man didn't respond, so Thabo shifted the body, using his knee and shoulder to leverage the dead weight over one shoulder, and managed to open the back door of the bald man's Merc, swearing profusely.

'Wait, what are you doing? Don't put that man in my car, are you crazy?' squeaked the bald man, pushing Thabo away and slamming the door of his Merc closed.

Thabo could no longer manage the weight of Uncle Mlungu. Staggering backwards, he dropped the body onto the tarmac with a thunk. Then he watched, open-mouthed, as the bald man ran around his idling Merc, leapt in and sped out of the parking lot with a squeal of tyres.

Thabo stood gaping at Uncle lying on the ground in front of the gusheshe. Then he turned to watch Papsak sprinting down the side of the dune, taking long strides, his arms waving wildly.

'What happened?' panted Papsak, skidding to a halt on the sandy tarmac, bending over, hands on his thighs.

'Crazy mlungu gave me the money, then left without Uncle. Quickly, let's get out of here.'

The two men scrambled into the gusheshe. Thabo laid his arm along the back of the passenger seat, looked over his shoulder, then put his foot flat down on the accelerator to reverse. There was a massive thump as the car lurched forward, hitting Uncle Mlungu hard.

'Fok!' Thabo shouted.

'What are you doing?' Papsak yelled back. 'Why are you running over Uncle Mlungu?'

'Shit shit! I thought the gusheshe was in reverse.' Thabo tugged at the gear stick, the cogs grinding as he forced the car into reverse, then surged backwards, clunking up onto the pavement and ramming the back of the gusheshe into a pole. Papsak flew forward, banging his head on the dashboard.

For a moment both men sat stunned as the car bounced off the pole and rolled forward, straight into Uncle Mlungu a second time, before coming to a creaking, crunching stop.

'Someone's coming, quick, drive, drive!' Papsak screamed.

Thabo looked round as a shabby man and woman, both in dirty yellow parking-guard vests ran into the car park, waving their arms and yelling.

'Drive!' Papsak shouted again.

Thabo put the car into gear, then rammed his foot down on the accelerator. There was a double thud as both the front right and back right tyres hit Uncle Mlungu again, and then they sped out of the parking lot, skidding as they tore down the road in the direction of Khayelitsha, the car making an ominous clunking noise.

'Are you okay?' Papsak asked.

'I think so,' Thabo responded. 'Is anyone following us?'

Papsak turned in his seat and looked out the back window. 'No, nobody,' he said. 'Why did you drive over Uncle Mlungu like that?' he asked.

'It was a mistake. I thought the car wanted to go backwards, but it wanted to go forwards.'

Papsak sat back in his seat and pulled on his seat belt, rubbing at the egg his clash with the dashboard had left on his forehead. 'Nentloko!' he mumbled.

Thabo pulled the Shoprite bag out of his jacket, and handed it to Papsak, who took three different goes to count the money. 'Fifteen thousand,' he said eventually with glee, just as smoke started pouring out the front of the gusheshe. There was another loud clunk from the engine, and a small fire began billowing from the bonnet.

Thabo pulled over on the deserted stretch of road. The two men took their shopping bag and started the long walk back to Khayelitsha, thumbs out for a ride.

THE PARAMEDICS

'Don't you think it's funny that they call this the graveyard shift? It makes no sense if you work in a button factory or something like that, but for us, I mean, it's creepy, don't you think?' Zayne was saying as the radio in the ambulance blurted to life through the static.

'Come in five nine indigo, reports of a hit-and-run at Strandfontein beach in the main parking lot,' the dispatcher's voice came through the radio.

'Copy that, five nine indigo, we're on our way,' S'bu said into the radio. 'Turn on the siren,' he told Zayne.

As Zayne pulled the ambulance into the parking lot between the dunes, he spotted two informal car guards standing beside a body flat on the tarmac. While Zayne parked and cut the sirens, S'bu raced over to the body.

'I thought you said he was still alive?' he said to the female car guard.

'I saw his finger move!' she protested.

'Hang on a minute. Hey Zayne, haven't we seen this body somewhere before?'

Zayne dropped to his haunches next to the body, which was not in the finest condition. 'No ways! Isn't that the Professor Noakes guy from our hijacked ambulance? What's he doing here?'

'Looks a little worse for wear. What have you been up to, buddy?' S'bu asked the dead body.

'Hey, do you still have that cop's card, the one from the crime scene, who grilled us after the hijack?'

'Yeah, hang on a sec, it's in my wallet. I'll get it and radio the mortuary.'

'We didn't do nothing,' said the male car guard. 'He was sommer like this when we found him.'

'Is there mos a reward?' asked his mate.

THE WIDOW

Maureen put her well-thumbed copy of *The Real Meal Revolution* on the table in a visible spot, to help Benjamin recognise her. Then she held the back of the spoon up to her face and checked the distorted reflection to make sure she didn't have lipstick on her teeth. She'd just had her nails done and her hair set; she'd made her hairdresser open early for her, thrown money at the problem. It was the first time in ages that she'd had her nails done. But now that there was this money pouring in from all the Tim Noakes ENDORSED Meal Plans she was selling, she figured she could afford to spend it however she wanted. She had earned it herself, after all.

She wasn't sure why she wanted to look good for Benjamin, or why she had butterflies in her tummy at the prospect of meeting him. Maybe it was because she was scared he'd see right through her, and know she was the fraudulent Lydia the second he laid eyes on her. Or perhaps it was because she was curious to see if his dark good looks online would translate into real life? She had to remind herself that she wasn't really Lydia (even though she sort of was); she was a sixty-year-old woman. And Benjamin would never, could never, look at her the way he would look at Lydia.

'Maureen?'

She looked up, startled at the sound of her own name. The man standing beside her table was in his late fifties, maybe. He was balding, with old-fashioned spectacles and a small paunch. He was neatly dressed in an expensive-looking suit, but he looked exhausted, and he hadn't shaved. Maureen searched her mind: maybe he was an old friend of Gus's from the office.

'I'm Benjamin,' said the newcomer, his face flushed with shame. 'It's nice to meet you.'

Maureen gaped, trying to reconcile the stocky little man standing in front of her with the Benjamin she knew online.

'I can explain,' he said, 'but I completely understand if you'd rather that I just went away.'

It took Maureen a moment to find her voice. She reminded herself that he was a potential client. 'No, please, sit, sit.'

'Thank you,' he said, sitting down gingerly.

'Forgive me, I don't know where my manners got to.'

'Please, let me explain...'

'No, really, you don't owe me any explanations.' Maureen stumbled over the words, trying to maintain her composure.

'But I want to explain, you have to allow me that if nothing else,' he said. Then the words came tumbling out of his mouth. 'You see I work, I mean I worked for a company that manufactures carbs: breads, croissants, cakes, sugary stuff, you know, contraband products,' he said, smiling to himself, recalling a private joke. Then cleared his throat and continued: 'Until very recently, I was the managing director of the company. If they'd known I was Banting – and successfully at that – and if they had any inkling that I'd joined a public Banting group on Facebook, the repercussions would have been severe. They would have fired me, and might have instigated legal proceedings. That's why I invented Benjamin. It was all so that I could join the group, and find a support system of wonderful like-minded people, like your friend Lydia and you, of course.'

'It's okay, Benjamin,' Maureen said.

'My real name is Trevor. Benjamin was my online pseudonym,' he said. 'And it's not okay. I've hurt people. I've been dishonest. I've done some terrible things, illegal things...'

Maureen looked at him closely. She could see that he was trying very hard not to cry. His bottom lip was quivering, and he couldn't bring himself to make eye contact. The thought struck Maureen that he was very much like her. It also occurred to her that he might actually be rather handsome, if he got a shave and a few good nights' sleep, and maybe dropped a couple of kilos.

Despite his deception, or perhaps due to her own, she felt deep empathy, as well as a desire to protect this poor broken man. She patted her hair with one hand. Then she covered his hand with her own. He looked up at her touch.

'It's really okay, Trevor,' she said. 'I think that everything is going to be okay.'

THE COP

'According to my autopsy, what we have here is a Caucasian male in his early to mid-sixties. Six foot three, eighty-one kilograms, mild male-pattern balding, almost all of his own teeth. Second stage of rigor was present. The body has extensive post-mortem injuries, which are consistent with an MVA,' the pathologist said.

'Which means what in English?' Bennie September asked.

'He seems to have been run over a number of times *after* he died.'

'So what was the cause of death?'

'Cause of death was asphyxia.'

'Oh, so he was strangled?'

'No, it was an obstruction in his trachea.'

'Meaning?' Bennie asked.

'He choked,' said the doctor. 'On what appears to be a piece of Ouma rusk.'

'So it wasn't murder?' Bennie couldn't believe what he was hearing.

'Nope, by the looks of things he was eating a rusk, and he choked on it.'

'But what about the cuts, the bruising and abrasions across his face and body?'

'Well, when he started choking on the bit of rusk, I suspect he panicked, and threw himself over the back of a chair to try and dislodge it. That kind of behaviour is consistent with injuries of this nature. When that didn't work, he may have bounced around the room in a panic, trying to bash the rusk out of his throat in other ways and with any household implements he could find, which would account for the broken nose, the blood, and the kinds of abrasions we see here.'

'Wait a minute, doctor. You're telling me that Professor Tim Noakes, the founder of the anti-carb movement, died choking on a rusk?' Bennie asked, incredulous.

'No, I'm not. It turns out that the deceased is not Professor Tim Noakes.'

'What?' Bennie said, spinning on his feet to face the doctor. 'Wait, let me get this straight. You mean this body does not belong to Tim Noakes?'

'They do share some physical attributes, but I can guarantee you, Detective September, the deceased is most definitely not Professor Tim Noakes.'

'How can you be so sure?' Bennie asked.

'Well, for a number of reasons. The first reason I believe this body does not belong to Professor Tim Noakes is because this man has a pacemaker. The second hint is that he has a tattoo of a very ample-bosomed woman on his left gluteus maximus. The third is that his fingerprints identify him as a fellow wanted for questioning in connection with a number of professional "hits". But the most compelling evidence that leads me to conclude that this body does not belong to Professor Tim Noakes,' said the doctor, taking his iPhone out his pocket, and brandishing it at the detective, 'is the fact that they just announced on News24 that Tim Noakes is alive and well, and has been at an ashram in the Karoo with his wife for the last seventy-two hours, without any contact with the outside world.'

Bennie took the iPhone and scrolled through the news story.

'The Prof contacted the press as soon as news of his death reached him,' the doctor said.

'Then where the hell did this guy come from?' Bennie asked, pointing at the body under a sheet on the table.

'No idea,' said the pathologist. 'But it appears that this time, he bit off more than he could chew.'

THE CO-AUTHORS

Marco opened a restaurant called Marco's Kitchen, where he serves fresh, homemade pasta, just like his nonna used to make, and her nonna before her, and her nonna before her. Professor Tim Noakes is a regular at Marco's Kitchen, where he particularly enjoys the Zoodles (noodles made out of zucchini) from the Banting section of the menu. He and Marco are still close, but no longer work together – although Marco did go to the launch of the Prof's new Mediterranean cookbook. He speaks to Shireen regularly, but is no longer in touch with Shaun or Xolisa.

Marco's still not a household name, but he's okay with that. He's also okay with the fact that he's ten kilos overweight. He and Chris have never been more in love, and are looking to adopt a child. *MasterChef South Africa* haven't asked him to be a judge yet, but fingers crossed.

Shireen lives in Johannesburg with her husband, two children, two dogs, three cats, and a hamster. Her Banting dietician practice continues to grow, and she is hard at work on a book called *The Banting Makeover: Hair and beauty tips for the LCHF lifestyle*. She calls Professor Noakes every day, just to make sure that he's okay.

After her divorce, **Xolisa** put on thirty-five kilos and started The South African Round and Proud Association, which urges women to love their bodies, no matter what their size. The SARPA website receives in the region of 15 000 hits per day. She is currently single, and not in contact with Prof Noakes or any of her other co-authors.

Shaun is still single and living in Cape Town. He is still a tool. He has no new books coming out.

THE WIDOW

Maureen Ewehout is now a bestselling author of romance novels. Her latest, *The Shropshire Lass and the Biker: The First of the Sarah Chronicles*, launches in a few weeks' time at The Book Lounge in Cape Town. She has removed herself from the Banting for Life Facebook page and has donated every cent she earned from her ENDORSED meal plans to The Noakes Foundation. She and Trevor live together in Rondebosch, with no cats.

THE EX-CEO

Trevor started his own company – a small artisanal bakery, located in the heart of Rondebosch, called Banting Buns. Maureen helped him formulate many of his unique recipes, including his trademarked cauli-bread. Last weekend the *Sunday Times* called Banting Buns a 'local treasure' and gave it four stars. Trevor is currently putting together a book of recipes.

THE EX-PUBLISHER

After going through intensive rehab and finding Jesus, **Frank** took up a position at CUM Books, where he discovered that publishing *could* be lucrative after all. On weekends he goes to Pollsmoor Prison, where he teaches inmates to read. He's also actively involved in a local campaign to abolish African Fiction sections from bookstores, promoting the idea that all fiction should be displayed together, in alphabetical order. His tell-all memoir, entitled *Two Nights in a South African Prison*, is due out at the end of this month.

Papsak is training to be a mortuary assistant; he has three more years to go before he is accredited. Last week Thabo bought him an Apple iPhone for his birthday.

Thabo started giving Real Meal Revolution low-carb, high-protein courses in the townships, which have become hugely successful. He has his own LCHF book coming out in all eleven vernaculars soon: *Banting Made Nca!* People call him the Tim Noakes of Khayelitsha. He is currently single, and drives a blue BMW three-series that he bought from a second-hand dealer (not Lefty).

Professor Noakes is alive and well, and continues to spread the word about the Banting lifestyle in between court cases and Twitter wars. Frank Collins continues sending him weekly care packages, filled with sugary treats, donuts, Ouma rusks and chocolate brownies, which remain unacknowledged, and may or may not have been responsible for the death of the first hitman.

The Prof recently launched his new book, which is already a bestseller. His publishers are very happy.

THE END

BULLETPROOF THANKS

This book was made with very few carbs and a great deal of love and support.

To Sarah Lotz, who has taught me more than I'll ever know, encouraged, advised, nurtured and inspired me: you're ace, and I'm beyond grateful.

My forever thanks goes to the early readers for their love and tough love: Sarah Lotz, Helen Moffett, Edyth Bulbring, Rahla Xenopolous, Fourie Botha, Karin Barry-McCormack, Rachel Zadok and Bongani Kona.

Ian Waddell, trainer to the stars (http://www.personalbest.co.za) for answering my billion and one questions about exercise.

Ruby Bunn and Ethan Gray, for all the information about the interior of ambulances and rigor mortis.

The wonderful and patient BookStorm team: Louise Grantham, Russell Clarke and Nicola van Rooyen.

The phenomenally talented professional book lovers who worked with such care and passion to make this book: Reneé Naudé and Karin Barry-McCormack. And Megan Clausen and Sophy Kohler, for extraordinary eagle-eyed proofing.

Warren McKnight for your unbreakable support.

Editor and friend extraordinaire, Helen Moffett: with each new project I work on with you, I can't believe my luck and your talent.

And of course, thanks to Professor Tim Noakes for having a great sense of humour and being such a good sport about this whole thing, particularly considering what happens to him on page one.

If you'd like to get in touch with me, please
join me on Facebook https://www.facebook.com/paige.nick.fans
find me on Twitter @paigen
or email me on amillionmilesfromnormal@gmail.com.

The incredible Noakes Foundation also deserves a shout-out: here's a bit about what they do.

Professor Tim Noakes and the Noakes Foundation are committed to world-class research through a large-scale research programme that addresses the scientific causes of the pandemics of obesity and type 2 diabetes. They are also flagshipping a community intervention programme that aims to help those with limited means learn to eat more healthily, heal themselves with their diets, and to feed their families and future generations in better ways.

Visit www.thenoakesfoundation.org
or contact info@thenoakesfoundation.org

If Banting has changed your life or the life of someone you know, please consider contacting the foundation to help sponsor someone with limited means to change theirs.

ALSO BY PAIGE NICK:

A Million Miles from Normal
This Way Up
Pens Behaving Badly

Writing as Helena S. Paige with Sarah Lotz and Helen Moffett, a series of choose-your-own-adventure erotic novels:

A Girl Walks into a Bar
A Girl Walks into a Wedding
A Girl Walks into a Blind Date

CPSIA information can be obtained at www.ICGtesting.com
Printed in the USA
LVOW10s0724281015

460004LV00002B/8/P